Table Of Contents

CHAPTER4:EQUIPMENT AND SUPPLIES USED IN PHLEBOTOMY 37

CHAPTER5: PERFORMING THE VENIPUNCTURE 55

Foreword

For more than three decades, Dr. Joel Siegal has been teaching students the Science of Phlebotomy. He has proudly trained thousands of Phlebotomy Technicians. Phlebotomy is more than just the art of drawing blood; it is an allied health field specialty that requires education, practical training, and sensitivity to patient needs. Every individual has had their blood drawn; for many, the Phlebotomist is one of the first caregivers they encounter. A positive experience with a Phlebotomist is often the stepping stone to the overall medical experience. A good Phlebotomist is essential to the overall success of patient care.

There are dozens of books on the topic of Phlebotomy. We found most of the books to be overly compressive, and meant more for medical students; or, we found they were not compressive enough to give adequate Phlebotomy Technician training. This book combines all the necessary elements for the training of phlebotomist to work in any health care setting. It has been written in an easy-to-read format, and covers the essentials needed for a successful career as a Phlebotomist.

As a health care provider you will be dealing with the sick, elderly and, disabled. It is up to you to show compassion and the highest level of respect to everyone you come in contact with. Remember, like yourself, the people you care for are also mothers, fathers, sons and daughters.

Dedication

This book is dedicated to my Mom and Dad, rest in piece.

Chapter 1

Introduction To Phlebotomy

Objectives

After completing this chapter, students should be able to:

- Define phlebotomy Identify the roles and responsibilities of a Phlebotomist
- Recognize the responsibility to their patients Recognize Phlebotomist's Code of Ethics
- Define Advanced Directives Define Patient's Rights

Glossary Terms

Confidentiality	Privacy regarding patient information.
Ethics	Standards of practice regarding behavior, developed as a result of one's concept of right and wrong.
Patient's Bill of Rights	A document created by the American Hospital Association that identifies privileges that patient in health care facilities are required to have.
Phlebotomist	An individual trained and skilled in collecting blood samples for clinical testing.
Phlebotomy	An invasion procedure in which a sharp object is inserted into the vein to obtain blood.
Professionalism	A group or traits or characteristics which display a positive image or code of ethics.

a. What is Phlebotomy?

Phlebotomy is the term used to describe the incision of a vein to collect blood. The word "phlebotomy" derives from the Greek words "phlebo", meaning "vein" and "tomy", meaning "to cut". The primary role of a phlebotomist is to collect and transport blood specimens for clinical laboratory analyses, using various techniques, including venipuncture and capillary puncture. A phlebotomist also assists in the collection and transportation of specimens other than venous blood specimens.

b. Phlebotomist Roles and Responsibilities

A phlebotomist:

- ✓ Identifies and prepares patients for blood collection procedures
- ✓ Collects blood specimens using correct venipuncture or capillary puncture technique
- ✓ Selects proper specimen containers
- ✓ Properly handles, labels and transports specimens
- ✓ Collects data and maintains records
- ✓ Performs computer operations where required
- ✓ Practices quality assurance procedures
- ✓ Follows departmental policies and procedures
- ✓ Maintains patient confidentiality
- ✓ Follows all safety regulations

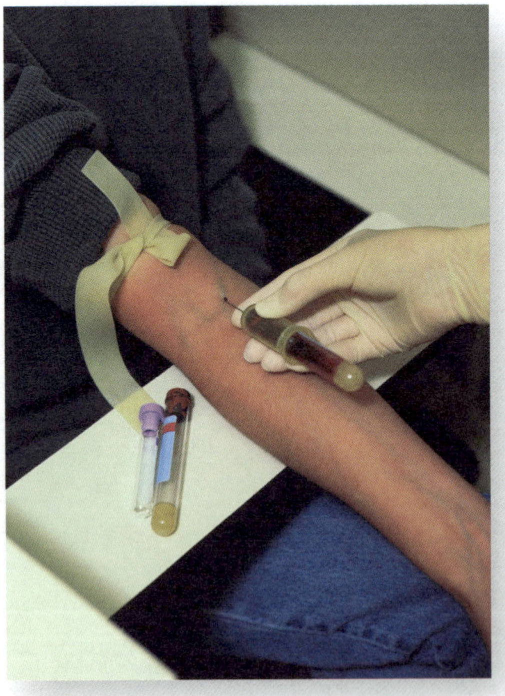

c. Your Responsibility to Patients

To inspire confidence:

- Have confidence in your own ability.
- Present a professional appearance to the patient.
- Demonstrate appropriate concern for the safety of the patient and yourself by following Standard Precautions.

To gain confidence in your ability:

- Know the proper techniques.
- Remember that increasing your experience will help you gain more confidence.
- Develop your patient communication skills.
- Understand that sometimes even the most skillful person will be unable to obtain a blood specimen. Do not be discouraged if you fail occasionally. Experience will help you improve your skills and develop your knowledge.
- Ask questions if you don't know the answer.

To present professionalism to your patient

- Maintain a calm attitude.
- Do not appear hurried.
- Make each patient feel important.
- Greet your patient with a warm smile.
- Practice good hygiene, including having clean hands and groomed nails. Artificial nails may be banned in some facilities.
- Wear gloves that fit appropriately.
- Following each blood collection, remove your gloves and use either an alcohol-based hand rub if hands are not visibly soiled or soap and water if hands are visibly soiled.
- Use new gloves for each patient.
- Dress conservatively. Your uniform, laboratory coat, and shoes should be clean, and your laboratory coat should be buttoned.
- Tie long hair back, otherwise it may contaminate the work area or the patient.

When approaching the patient:

1. Introduce yourself.
2. Identify the patient.
3. Gain the patient's confidence by explaining what you are going to do.
4. Reassure the patient and try to reduce any stress or tension which they may be experiencing.

d. Phlebotomist's Code of Ethics

Following a code of ethics is a principal part of being a phlebotomist. Ethics consists of a set of rules, regulations, or guidelines that examines values, actions, and choices to help determine what is right vs. wrong. Prior to drawing blood, in addition to asking the patient to state his or her name, the phlebotomist is required to properly indentify the patient by checking the armband and other qualifying information, such as the requisition form. Obtaining blood for the incorrect patient constitutes an act of negligence and can result in disciplinary action.

Ethics also involves confidentiality and privacy of patient information. Phlebotomists are required to practice discretion and confidentiality at all times. Confidentiality is especially important in regards to the patient's diagnosis and prognosis. Many times, family members may ask when blood will be drawn, or other questions pertaining to the patient. It is the responsibility of the physician, not the phlebotomist, to discuss this information with the patient. All patient information must remain confidential to project both the patient as well as the facility. A phlebotomist should never disclose confidential patient information such as a laboratory result. Doing so is a breach of patient confidentiality and may be subject to disciplinary or legal action.

e. Advanced Directives

Advance directives are legal documents that allow patients to communicate their decisions about end-of-life ahead of time. They provide a way for patients to express their wishes to family, friends and health care professionals. Advanced Directives may include a living will and a medical power of attorney. A living will allows a patient to document his or her wishes concerning medical treatments at the end-of-life. A medical power of attorney allows a patient to select a person whom they trust to make health care decisions for them on their behalf.

In the event that blood specimens are required for examination after harm or death occurs in a patient, the collection and examination process requires the knowledge and skills of a competent phlebotomist. From the time the physician writes the patient order for blood collection, until the time the analysis of the specimens occur, the phlebotomist is the main guardian of the quality of the specimen.

f. Patient Rights

Patient's Bill of Rights
Source: New York State Department of Health
http://www.health.state.ny.us/professionals/patients/patient_rights/

As a patient in a hospital in New York State, patients have the right, consistent with law, to:

(1) Understand and use these rights. If for any reason you do not understand or you need help, the hospital MUST provide assistance, including an interpreter.
(2) Receive treatment without discrimination as to race, color, religion, sex, national origin, disability, sexual orientation, source of payment, or age.
(3) Receive considerate and respectful care in a clean and safe environment free of unnecessary restraints.
(4) Receive emergency care if you need it.
(5) Be informed of the name and position of the doctor who will be in charge of your care in the hospital.
(6) Know the names, positions and functions of any hospital staff involved in your care and refuse their treatment, examination or observation.
(7) A no smoking room.
(8) Receive complete information about your diagnosis, treatment and prognosis.
(9) Receive all the information that you need to give informed consent for any proposed procedure or treatment. This information shall include the possible risks and benefits of the procedure or treatment.
(10) Receive all the information you need to give informed consent for an order not to resuscitate. You also have the right to designate an individual to give this consent for you if you are too ill to do so. If you would like additional information, please ask for a copy of the pamphlet "Do Not Resuscitate Orders — A Guide for Patients and Families."
(11) Refuse treatment and be told what effect this may have on your health.
(12) Refuse to take part in research. In deciding whether or not to participate, you have the right to a full explanation.
(13) Privacy while in the hospital and confidentiality of all information and records regarding your care.
(14) Participate in all decisions about your treatment and discharge from the hospital. The hospital must provide you with a written discharge plan and written description of how you can appeal your discharge.
(15) Review your medical record without charge. Obtain a copy of your medical record for which the hospital can charge a reasonable fee. You cannot be denied a copy solely because you cannot afford to pay.
(16) Receive an itemized bill and explanation of all charges.
(17) Complain without fear of reprisals, about the care and services you are receiving, and to have the hospital respond to you and if you request it, a written response. If you are not satisfied with the hospital's response, you can complain to the New York State Health Department. The hospital must provide you with the State Health Department telephone number.
(18) Authorize those family members and other adults who will be given priority to visit consistent with your ability to receive visitors.
(19) Make known your wishes in regard to anatomical gifts. You may document your wishes in your health care proxy or on a donor card, available from the hospital.

Public Health Law(PHL)2803 (1)(g)Patient's Rights, 10NYCRR, 405.7,405.7(a)(1),405.7(c)

Chapter 1 – Review Questions

MULTIPLE CHOICE:

Select the best response for each of the following questions.

1. _________________ is used to describe a group or traits or characteristics which display a positive image or code of ethics.

   a. disciplinary
   b. confidentiality
   c. professionalism
   d. mannerism

2. _________________ are legal documents that allow patients to communicate their decisions about end-of-life ahead of time.

   a. patient directives
   b. advance directives
   c. confidential directives
   d. medical will

WORD SCRAMBLE:

Unscramble the word to fill in the blank:

3. **hleosttopmib**

   A _________________ is an individual trained and skilled in collecting blood samples for clinical testing.

4. **tiechs**

   _________________ are standards of practice regarding behavior, developed as a result of one's concept of right and wrong.

5. **pnearapace**

   To inspire confidence, present a professional _________________ to the patient.

6. **rienpxeece**

   To gain confidence, _________________ will help you improve your skills and develop your knowledge.

TRUE OR FALSE:

Indicate if the following statements are True or False.

7. _______ The word "phlebotomy" derives from the Greek words "phlebo", meaning "vein" and "tomy", meaning "to cut".

8. _______ The Patient's Bill of Rights is a series of laws created by the government that identifies privileges that patient in health care facilities are required to have.

FILL IN THE BLANKS:

Write the word(s) or statement needed to answer the following questions:

9. Name at least 5 responsibilities of a phlebotomist:

____

____

____

____

____

10. When approaching the patient, what should you say or do? List the 4 steps below.

____

____

____

____

Chapter 2

Health Care Facilities And The Clinical Laboratory

Objectives

After completing this chapter, students should be able to:

- Identify all hospital departments and functions
- Recognize the different departments and subunits of a Clinical Laboratory
- Recognize the different types of personnel of a Clinical Laboratory

Glossary Terms

Hospital	An institution which provides medical, surgical or psychiatric care and treatment for the sick or injured.
Hospital Department	A division of a hospital specializing in a particular area or service pertaining to the medic al field.
Inpatient	A patient who is admitted to a hospital for treatment requiring at least one overnight stay.
Outpatient	A patient who visits a hospital or clinic for treatment requiring no overnight stay.
Physician Specialization	An area of treatment and study by a physician who is specialized and possesses advanced knowledge and education in that field.
Surgical Specialty	A surgical procedure pertaining to a specific medical topic. For example: autopsy, biopsy, etc.
Nursing Services	Includes a wide variety of services provided by nursing individuals including hospital staffing, nurses, home health aides, private duty nurses, and elder care.

As a member of a health care system, a phlebotomist is required to have an understanding of the health care environment. Clinical laboratories can be located within a hospital, as part of a physician's office, within a clinic, or as an independent laboratory.

a. Health Care Facilities

11.) Hospital

The hospital is the focal point of a large part of health care in the United States. Although a patient's primary care is delivered in a physician's office, the hospital treats acute illnesses, conducts surgical procedures, trains and educates health care professionals, conducts research, provides outpatient services, and provides educational resources to the public. Some hospitals have trauma centers which treats victims of accidents. Table 2.1 lists departments found in most hospital and medical centers. Table 2.2 lists Physicians Specializations, Surgical Specialties and Nursing Services.

Table 2.1 Hospital Departments

Anesthesiology	Administers local and general drugs to obtain a complete or partial loss of feeling during an invasive procedure such as surgery.
Clinical Laboratory	Performs various tests on blood, tissues and other specimens. Also processes and analyzes specimens and maintains a database of results.
Coronary Care Unit or Cardiac Care Unit (CCU)	Treats and provides care for seriously ill heart patients.
Diagnostic Imaging	Performs X-ray-related procedures including magnetic resonance imaging (MRI) and computerized axial tomography (CAT) scans.
Emergency Room (ER) or Emergency Department (ED)	Provides immediate treatment for seriously ill and injured patients with medical emergencies.
Infection Control	Identifies, controls and educates staff about infectious diseases.
Intensive Care Unit (ICU)	Treats and provides care for seriously ill and injured patients; ICU's can be found in special areas, such as pediatric ICU, neonatal intensive care (NICU), medical ICU, surgical ICU and coronary care unit (CCU).
Internal Medicine	Diagnoses and treats patients with general medical conditions.
Labor and Delivery (L&D)	Treats women during the birth process; L&D is separate from the nursery and postpartum area.
Nuclear Medicine	Uses radioactive isotopes in the diagnosis and treatment of disease.
Nursing Services	Provides direct care to ill and injured patients including administering medications.
Obstetrics (OB)	Provides care for mothers and newborns throughout the birth process including labor, delivery, postpartum, and nursery.
Occupational Therapy (OT)	Uses different techniques to assist mentally and physically challenged patients to return to activities of daily living.
Oncology	Provides care and treatment of cancer patients.
Outpatient (OP)	Provides care for patients who are not hospitalized.
Pediatrics	Treats and provides health care for infants and children.
Pharmacy	Prepares and dispenses patient medications.

Table 2.1 Hospital Departments *(continued)*	
Physical Therapy (PT)	Provides treatments and therapies to correct disabilities and restore mobility.
Pulmonary Medicine	Diagnoses and treats respiratory disorders.
Psychiatry	Diagnoses and treats emotional disorders.
Radiation Therapy	Uses radioactive substances for the diagnosis and treatment of disease.
Radiology	Uses radioactive substances and visualization (x-ray) techniques for the diagnosis and treatment of disease.
Respiratory Therapy (RT)	Treats pulmonary (lung) disorders and diseases.
Social Services	Assists patients in referrals to other health care facilities such as nursing homes and home health care.
Surgery	Diagnoses and treats patients using an invasive surgical procedure.

Table 2.2 Physician Specializations, Medical Specialties	
Adolescent Medicine	Treats patients ages 11 to 21.
Allergy and Immunology	Treats abnormal responses or acquired hypersensitivity to substances with medical methods including testing and desensitization.
Anesthesiology	Administers local and general drugs to induce loss of consciousness and/or sensation during an invasive procedure.
Cardiology	Treats cardiovascular disorders and diseases.
Dermatology	Treats injuries and diseases relating to the skin.
Family Practice	Treats entire family regardless of members' ages.
Geriatric Medicine (Gerontology)	Focuses on care and diseases of the elderly.
Hematology	Studies blood and blood-forming tissues.
Infection Control	Prevents and treats infectious diseases.
Internal Medicine	Treats adult patients with medical problems such as high blood pressure and heart disease.
Nephrology	Treats disorders and diseases of the kidney.
Neurology	Treats non-surgical patients with diseases or disorders of the nervous system.
Obstetrics (OB) and Gynecology (GYN)	Treats women through pregnancy and delivery and disorders of the reproductive system.
Oncology	Studies cancer and cancer-related tumors.
Ophthalmology	Treats disorders of the eye.
Orthopedics	Prevents and corrects disorders of the musculoskeletal system.
Otorhinolaryngology or Ear, Nose, & Throat (ENT)	Medically and surgically treats ear, nose, and throat diseases.
Pathology	Specializes in diagnosing the abnormal changes in tissues that are removed during surgery.
Pediatrics	Provides medical care of children from birth to maturity.
Physical Medicine or Rehabilitative Medicine	Treats patients after they have suffered an injury or disability.
Preventive Medicine	Prevents physical and mental illness or disability.
Psychiatry	Treats/diagnoses mental, behavioral, or emotional disorders.
Radiology	Studies tissue and organs based on X-ray visualization.
Rheumatology	Treats disorders/diseases caused by inflammation of the joints.

Table 2.2 Physician Specializations, Surgical Specialties	
Cardiovascular	Surgically treats the heart and blood vessels.
Colorectal	Surgically treats the lower intestinal tract (colon and rectum).
Cosmetic or Plastic Surgery	Reconstructs underlying tissues to correct defects or remove scars.
Neurosurgery	Surgically treats diseases and disorders of the central nervous system.
Oral (Periodontics, Orthodontics)	Uses incision and surgery to treat disorders of the teeth, gums, and jaws.

Table 2.2 Physician Specializations, Nursing Services	
Orthopedic	Treats musculoskeletar injuries and disorders, congenital, deformities, and spinal curvatures through surgical means.
Thoracic	Surgically treats disorders and diseases of the chest.
Nurse Practitioner (NP)	Registered nurse (RN) who has received additional training such as in community health or pediatrics.
Registered Nurse (RN)	Provides direct patient care, teaches and supervises other staff, receives education and training in a diploma program, .a 2-yr. or 4-yr. program; takes state exam to become licensed.
Licensed Practical Nurse (LPN)	Able to perform some of the same tasks as a registered nurse; receives education in a 1- to 2-year program.
Certified Nursing Assistant (CNA)	Patient care attendant who provides patient care (bathing/feeding the patient, checking vital signs) under the supervision of a nurse

b. Support Services Departments

In addition to the main departments in a hospital, there are also many support services departments who handle accounting and business office functions, billing and collection, data processing, medical records and registration. There are also support services departments which handle human resources, food service, security, purchasing, maintenance and housekeeping.

c. Clinical Laboratory

The clinical laboratory is comprised of many departments as well as health care professionals. Table 2.3 lists clinical laboratory departments, and table 2.4 lists clinical subunit departments.

Table 2.3 Clinical Laboratory Departments	
Chemistry	is filled with fascinating, state-of-the-art technology which helps laboratory professionals to quickly analyze the chemical composition of blood and body fluids. Some of the tests performed in the chemistry section include glucose testing (aids in the diagnosis of diabetes), cholesterol, and drug testing.
Cytology	is the study of human cells. This is where cell samples are examined to detect early signs of cancer and other diseases. One of the principle functions is the detection of cancer of the cervix (the familiar "PAP" smear).
Hematology	counts, describes and identifies cells in blood and other body fluids. The slightest change in shape or size or number of cells will tell these skilled laboratory professionals if you are anemic or have leukemia.
Histology	evaluates cells in tissues and organs. The histotechnologist also helps the pathologist with such complex tasks as fine needle biopsies (a special procedure that collects tissue from lesions) and autopsies (to determine the cause of death).
Immunology	is the study of the body's response to viruses or allergy-causing agents. This area is responsible for many tests of the efficiency of the human immune system.
Data Entry	coordinates all the activities that keep the laboratory operation running smoothly and efficiently. Dedicated personnel look up test results for physicians and nurses, send reports to nursing station, order outpatient's lab work and perform all the clerical duties.
Microbiology	tracks down and identifies disease-causing bacteria, parasites or viruses. These laboratory professionals will use growth characteristics in artificial media, chemical testing and slide identification to determine which medications will work against the infections.
Phlebotomy	is the collection and processing of blood and other specimens. After processing, the samples are distributed to different areas of the laboratory for analysis.
Transfusion Medicine or Blood Bank	supplies all the blood products that are necessary for the treatment of many types of blood disorders including anemia and blood clotting disorders. Each blood unit is individually typed for blood group, screened for antibodies and tested for contagious diseases.

Printed with permission of St. Luke's Regional Medical Center

Table 2.4 Clinical Subunit Departments	
Clinical Analysis	Summary of Tests Performed
Clinical Chemistry	Total proteins, glucose and glucose tolerance, total cholesterol, triglycerides, hemoglobin high-density lipoprotein HDL cholesterol, electrolytes, magnesium, creatinine, uric acid, BUN, blood gases, enzymes, bilirubin and liver function tests, hormone tests, and drug analysis
Hematology and Coagulation	Differential, hemoglobin, eosinophil, hematocrit, CBC, fibrinogen, LE preparation, platelets, RBC, sedimentation rate, PTT, PT, WBC, and reticulocyte count
Microbiology	Gram staining, occult blood in the stool, blood culture, AFB, pinworm test, ova and parasites (Q&P), stool culture, strep screen, urine culture, culture and sensitivity, C&S, nose and throat culture.
Blood Bank	Blood typing, hepatitis antigen and antibody tests, cross matching test, and Coombs test.
Immunology and Serology	Rubella titer, Venereal Disease Research Laboratory (VDRL), salmonella agglutinins, rheumatoid testing (RA), C-reactive proteins, mononucleosis tests, and ASO titer for Streptococcus.
Urinalysis	Specific gravity, pH, glucose [sugar], protein, ketones, nitrites, bilirubin, urobilinogen, occult blood, and leukocytes (WBC).
Surgical and Anatomical Pathology	
Autopsy tests	Examination of tissues and organs to aid in determining cause of death.
Surgical Biopsy on Histology	Examination of tissue samples removed during surgery.
Cytology	Specimens observed for cancer detection (e.g., PAP test).

d. Phlebotomy Communication Networks

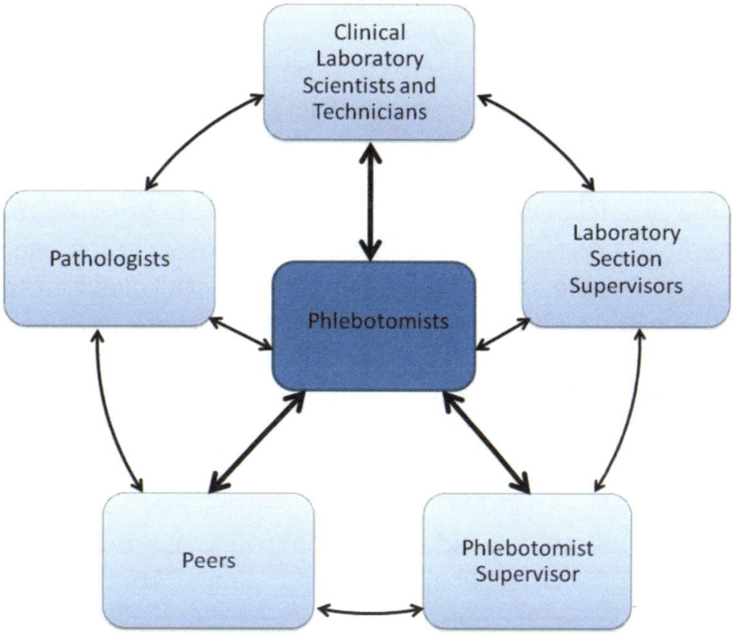

Figure 2.1 Phlebotomy Laboratory Communication Network.

The heavier lines indicate more frequent communication pathways.

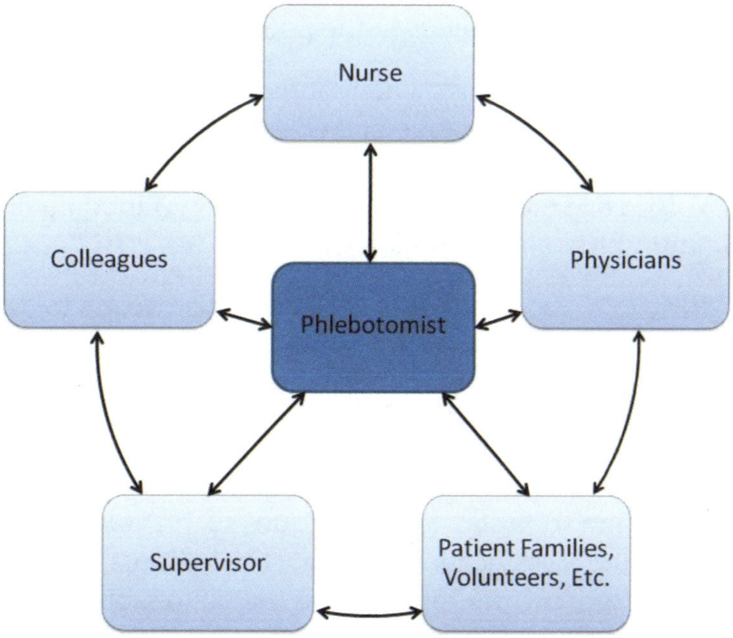

Figure 2.2 A phlebotomist's hospital communication network.

e. Clinical Pathology Personnel

12.) The Pathologists

A pathologist is a special type of doctor that participates in your day-to-day hospital care by providing and interpreting laboratory information. This information is used to help solve diagnostic problems and monitor the effects of therapy.

A pathologist is a physician who took four or more years of additional training after completing medical school in order to become an expert in the use of laboratory tests to diagnose and treat disease. Because of the pathologist's role in interpreting test results and in research, he or she is sometimes called "the doctor's doctor."

The pathologist is a physician and reads and interprets the results of laboratory test or examines tissues under a microscope to diagnose and monitor disease. They are licensed medical doctors (MDs) who are experts in diagnosing such diseases as cancer, diabetes, AIDS, hepatitis and thyroid conditions. The American Board of Pathology requires five years of training following graduation from medical school to be eligible to take examinations leading to Board certification as a Clinical/Anatomic Pathologist.

13.) The Technologists

Technologists are highly skilled professionals possessing the knowledge and training to assist the pathologist discover what is wrong (or right) with a patient. Technologists perform a full range of laboratory tests - from simple, pre-marital blood tests to complex tests that detect cancer. Technologists are also responsible for confirming the accuracy of test results and reporting the findings to the pathologist and other doctors.

A Medical Technologist (MT) - Holds a minimum of a baccalaureate degree and is responsible for performing a full range of laboratory tests, confirming the accuracy of test results, and reporting laboratory findings to the pathologist and other physicians. Medical technologists work in five major areas of the laboratory: blood banking, chemistry, hematology, immunology and microbiology.

A Cytotechnologist (CT) - Examines cells under the microscope to detect signs of cancer in the earliest stages when a cure is most likely. Cytotechnologists must hold baccalaureate degrees and have special training to search out the smallest abnormalities in color, shape or sizes of cells.

A Histotechnologist (HTL) - Prepares body tissue samples for microscopic examination by the pathologist using sophisticated techniques such as electron microscopy and immunohistochemistry. Histotechnologists must hold baccalaureate degrees and have special training to freeze, cut, mount and stain the tissues, often while the patient is still in surgery, thus playing a major role in the diagnosis of malignancy.

14.) The Technicians

Medical Laboratory Technicians are an important part of the health care team. Special types of technicians include the histologic technician (prepares tiny sections of body tissues for microscopic examinations by a pathologist) and the phlebotomy technician (collects blood samples for laboratory analysis).

A Phlebotomy Technician (PBT) - Collects blood samples to be used in many laboratory tests to detect disease and monitor treatment. Phlebotomists have special training often obtained at technical career training facilities and may go on to take a national certification exam in the area of phlebotomy. Phlebotomist Technicians are an integral member of the health care team.

Chapter 2 – Review Questions

MULTIPLE CHOICE:

Select the best response for each of the following questions.

1. _________________ is used to describe a division of a hospital specializing in a particular area or service pertaining to the medical field.

   e. specialization
   f. department
   g. institution
   h. administration

2. _________________ is the area of a hospital which provides direct care to ill and injured patients including administering medications.

   e. pharmacy
   f. support services
   g. nursing services
   h. infection control

WORD SCRAMBLE

Unscramble the word to fill in the blank:

3. **alsphoit**

   A _________________ is institution which provides medical, surgical or psychiatric care and treatment for the sick or injured.

4. **tietnnpia**

   An _________________ is patient who is admitted to a hospital for treatment requiring at least one overnight stay.

TRUE OR FALSE:

Indicate if the following statements are true or false.

5. _______ Physician Specialization is an area of treatment and study by a physician who is specialized and possesses advanced knowledge and education in that field.

6. _______ Hematology is the study of blood and blood-forming tissues.

7. _______ A Certified Nursing Assistant (CNA) provides direct patient care, teaches and supervises other staff, receives education and training in a diploma program, .a 2-yr. or 4-yr. program; takes state exam to become licensed.

8. _______ Microbiology tracks down and identifies disease-causing bacteria, parasites or viruses.

FILL IN THE BLANKS:

Write the word(s) or statement needed to answer the following questions:

9. Name at least 3 Clinical Laboratory Departments:

____

____

____

____

____

10. List one member of Clinical Pathology Personnel and explain their role.

____

____

____

Chapter 3

The Circulatory System And Its Relationship To Phlebotomy

Objectives

After completing this chapter, students should be able to:

- Describe the cardiovascular system (circulatory system)
- Identify the chambers of the heart
- Define the three types of blood vessels
- Identify the veins of the arms/hand List the cellular elements of blood
- Describe the major components of red blood cells, white blood cells, and platelets

Glossary Terms

Aerobic	Lives in the presence of oxygen.
Anaerobic	Able to live without oxygen.
Anemia	Deficiency of red blood cells, hemoglobin, or both.
Antibody	A protective body protein that is produced as a result to exposure to an antigen, or foreign bodies, such as bacteria or virus.
Anticoagulant	A substance that delays or prevents blood from clotting.
Antigen	A substance that stimulates a specific resistance response and thus causes the body to produce antibodies.
Aorta	The largest artery in the body.
Arteriole	The smallest of the arteries.
Basophils	Least numerous type of leukocyte that releases histamine and heparin to damaged tissues.
Cardiovascular	Pertaining to the heart and blood vessels.
Clot	Coagulated blood.
Coagulation	The stopping of bleeding, or clot formation.
Coumadin	An anticoagulant or blood thinning agent also known as warfarin; prothrombin time determination are essential for its proper control.
Cyanosis	A condition in which the skin turns a bluish color caused by lack of oxygen to the blood.
deoxygenated	Containing a higher concentration of carbon dioxide than oxygen.
differential	A percentage of each type of white blood cell in a total of 100 white cells observed.

eosinophil	Leukocyte that aids the body in fighting parasites which occurs in increased number in patients with allergies.
fibrin	Threadlike strains of protein formed by the action of thrombin on fibrinogen.
fibrinogen	Protein found in plasma which is essential for clotting of blood.
hemoglobin	A complex protein that carries oxygen from the lungs to the tissues.
hematology	The study of blood and its diseases.
hemophilia	A hereditary disease characterized by a prolonged clotting time of the blood.
hemorrhage	Abnormal internal or external bleeding.
hemostatis	Process of coagulation, or clot formation, that repairs vessel damage and stops blood loss.
hemotoma	Collection of blood under the skin due to leakage of blood from a punctured vein or artery.
homeostasis	The body's ability to attain a steady state.
hormone	A substance that is produced by a ductless gland and is carried to other parts of the body by the blood; it exerts control over many of the body's processes.
hyperglycemia	Excessive amount of sugar in the blood.
hyperkalemia	An excess in the amount of potassium in the blood.
hyperlipidemia	A term meaning an excess of any or all kinds of lipids in the plasma.
hypernatremia	Excess of sodium in the blood.
hypoglycemia	Decreased sugar level in the blood.
hypokalemia	Decreased potassium in the blood.
hyponatremia	Decreased sodium in the blood.
leukocyte	White blood cell whose main function is fighting infection and removing disintegrating tissues.
leukocytosis	An increase in the number of white blood cells.
leuckopenia	A decrease in the number of white blood cells.
lysis	The dissolution of a red blood cell.
lymphoctye	Leukocyte that multiplies in the lymphoid tissue and has a role in the body's immune system.
monocyte	Large leukocyte formed in bone marrow that ingests bacteria, old red blood cells, and debris in tissues.
neutrophil	Leukocyte that surrounds and digests pathogens found in tissue.
oxygenated	Containing a higher concentration of oxygen than carbon dioxide.
phagocytosis	Process by which bacteria and antigens are surrounded by leukocytes.
phlebitis	Inflammation of a vein, often accompanied by clot formation.
plasma	Clear, pale yellow fluid component of blood that contains fibrinogen.
pulmonary	Refers to the lungs and lung tissue.
serology	The testing of blood serum for antigen-antibody reaction.
serum	Clear, pale, yellow fluid that remains when blood is allowed to clot and that does not contain fibrinogen; plasma without the clotting factors.
syncope	A fainting spell.
thrombocyte	Also called a platelet; the smallest of the formed elements in the bloodstream.
thrombophlebitis	Inflammation of the wall of a vein with an accompanying clot at the site.
thrombosis	The formation of a blood clot is called a thrombus, which remains at the site of its formation in the circulatory system; when it becomes detached, it is known as an embolus.
vein	Blood vessel that carries deoxygenated blood from body tissues back to the heart.
vein cava	The largest vein in the body.
venule	A very small vein.

a. Introduction to the Circulatory System

It is important for the phlebotomist to possess a firm understanding of blood's functionality and composition. In addition, the phlebotomist must understand how blood vessels transport blood throughout the body. In order to perform venipuncture properly, the phlebotomist must also be able to identify the most commonly used veins in the arm.

b. Heart Chambers

The circulatory system is composed of the heart and blood vessels. The heart pumps blood through blood vessels. There are four chambers in the heart: two atrial, or upper chambers, and two ventricles, or lower chambers. The chambers are divided into right and left sides by walls called septa. The right atrium receives deoxygenated blood from various parts of the body, primarily by two veins called the superior vena cava and the inferior vena cava. The superior vena cava carries blood from the body parts superior to, or above the heart. The inferior vena cava carries blood from the body parts inferior to, or below the heart.

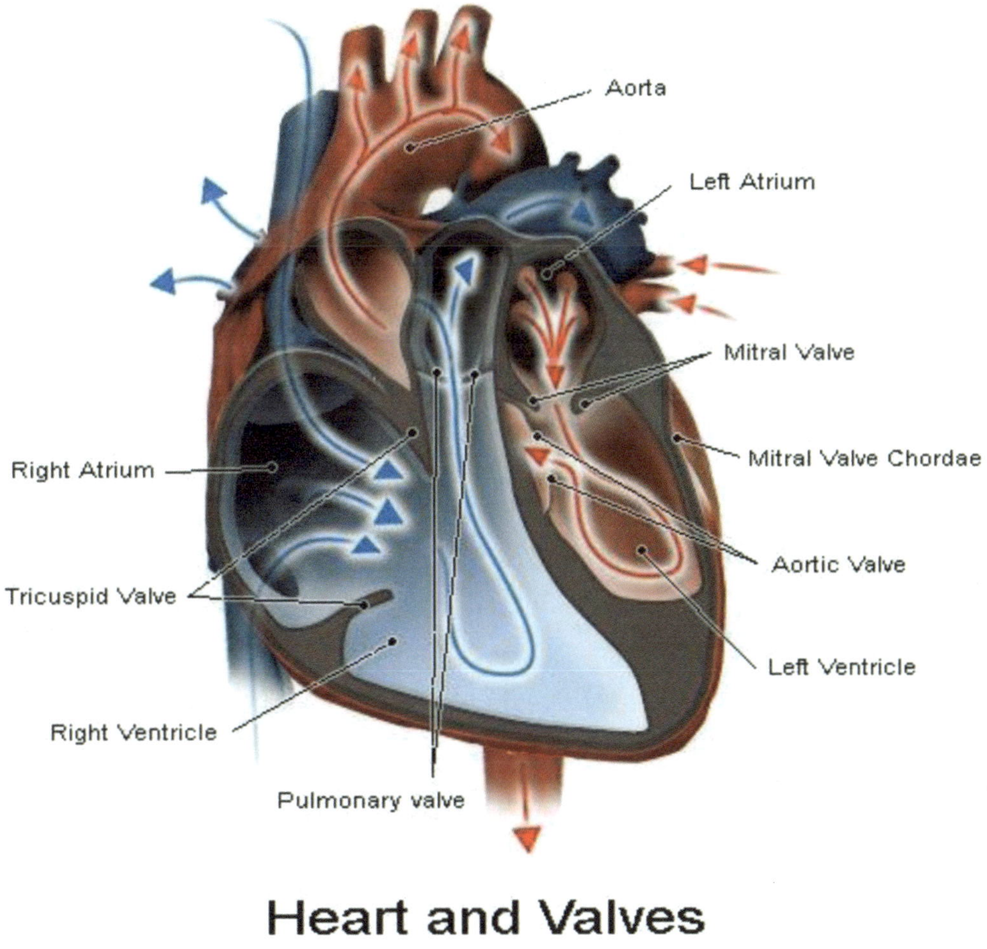

Figure 3.1 The Heart and Large Vessels

c. The Circulation of Blood (Cardiovascular System)

The blood flows from the right atrium to the right ventricle, and pumps it to the lungs. In the lungs, the blood releases carbon dioxide and picks up oxygen. The oxygenated blood returns to the left atrium in the heart, and then passes to the left ventricle and out of the heart. It is then distributed via the aorta, the largest artery, to circulate throughout the body. The pattern of blood flow is maintained by valves within the heart's chambers. The four values in the heart are: the tricuspid, mitral, pulmonary, and aortic semilunar.

The circulation of blood is essential to homeostasis and to sustaining life.

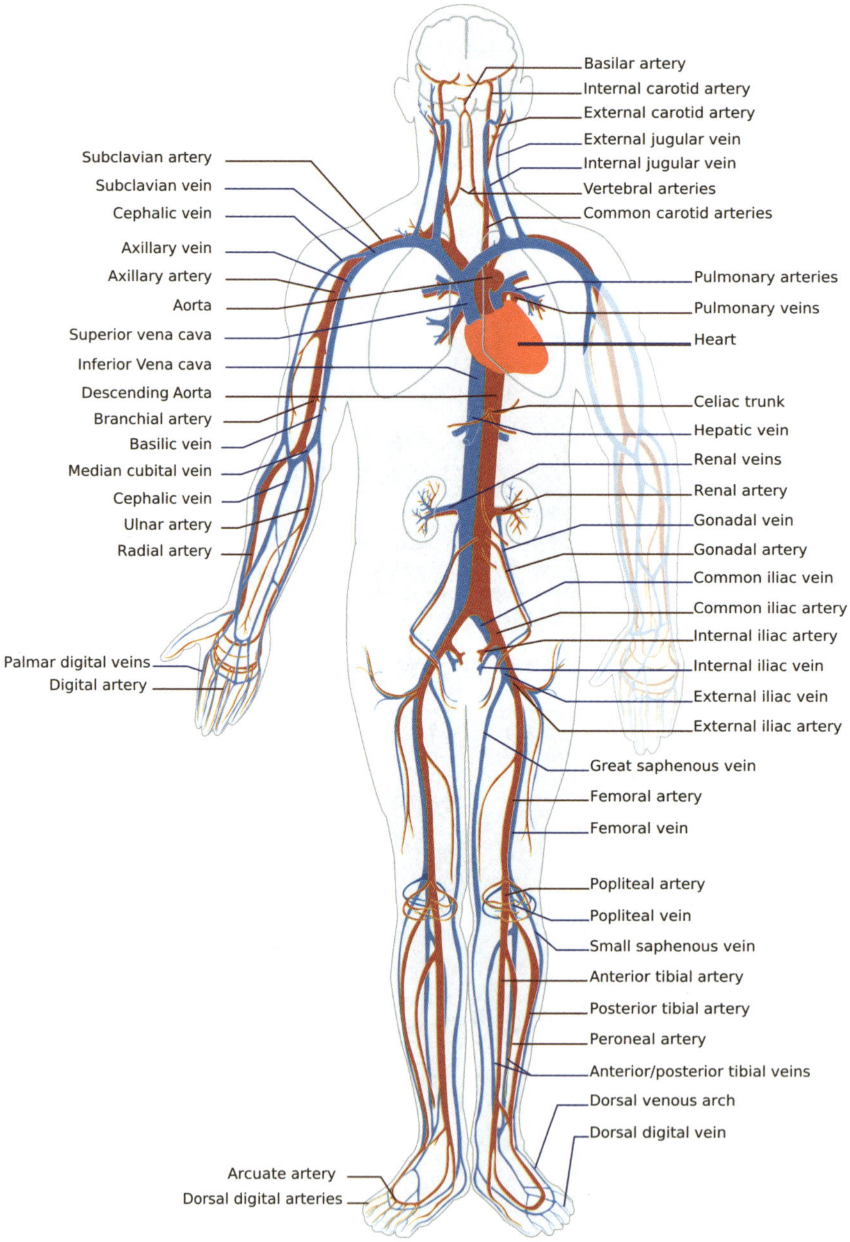

Figure 3.2 The Circulatory System

d. Blood Vessels

There are three types of blood vessels: arteries, veins and capillaries.

1.) Arteries

carry oxygenated blood away from the heart. This includes all arteries in the human body except for the pulmonary and umbilical arteries, which carry unoxygenated blood to the lungs and placenta. Smaller arteries are called arterioles.

2.) Capillaries

are very small and narrow, and are connecting units between the arteries and veins. They carry oxygen-rich blood from the arteries to the cells in the body. Capillaries are an important part of circulation because through their walls, oxygen, nutrients, and waste products pass between the blood and cells.

3.) Veins

carry deoxygenated blood toward the heart. They are composed of three layers of tissue, but their walls are very fine. Veins are smaller and much thinner than arteries. Blood pressure in the veins is also much lower than in the arteries. The smallest of the veins of called venules.

e. Superficial Veins of Arm/Hand

The major veins in the arm that a phlebotomist should be familiar with are the basilic, cephalic and median cubital. These veins, which are closer to the surface, are superficial in this area and are referred to as antecubital veins. They are the three major arm veins used venipuncture. Superficial veins are often easily to feel and locate for blood collection purposes. The deeper veins, such as the brachial vein, may be more difficult to feel and locate.

The most commonly used veins for venipuncture are located in the middle of the arms and in front of the elbow. The median cubital is usually large and easy to locate. It is the best choice for venipuncture and will cause the least pain to the patient. The cephalic and basilica veins may be used, but they may not be as easy to locate. Phlebotomists must be careful to not inadvertently puncture the median nerve, which can be quite painful to the patient.

Other sites for venipuncture include veins in the back of the hand, which are used when the antecubital veins are not accessible. Hand veins are smaller and less anchored. They may also be more painful for patient.

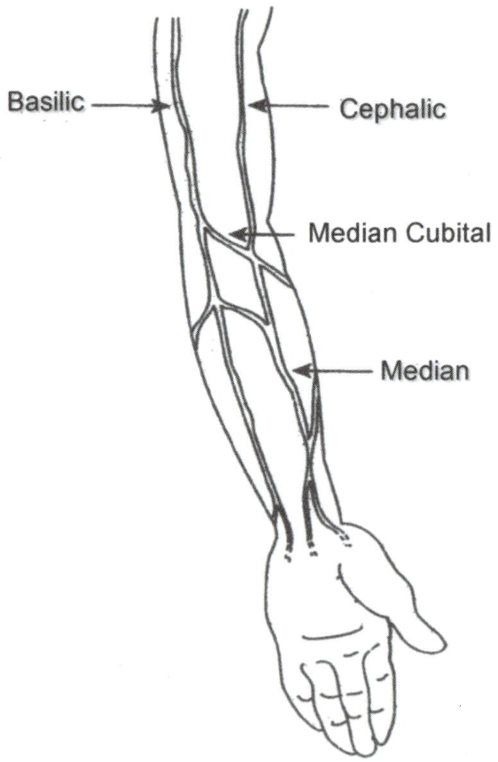

Figure 3.3 Veins in the Arm

f. Blood Components

1.) What is Blood?

Blood is a substance which flows through the arteries and veins. It carries oxygen and nutrients to the tissues, and carbon dioxide and waste products from the tissues. Blood consists of a liquid component called plasma, and a cellular component, which includes red blood cells, white blood cells and platelets. Plasma makes up about 55% of total blood volume. The other 45% are the formed elements or cells.

Plasma is approximately 90% water. The other 10% is made up of minerals, foods, wastes, hormones, antibodies, enzymes, and proteins, including those used to clot blood. When blood is allowed to clot in a tube, the liquid is called serum. Serum does not contain the proteins used for the blood to clot.

2.) The Three Types of Blood Cells

Blood cells originate mostly from the bone marrow inside of bones, and develop into three types. The formation of blood cells begins during fetal development. All blood cells originate from the hematopoietic stem cell but mature into individual cells. The three classes of blood cells are erythrocytes (red blood cells), leukocytes (white blood cells), and thrombocytes (platelets).

3.) Erythrocytes Maturation (Red Blood Cells)

The largest cellular portion of blood consists of erythrocytes, or RBC's (red blood cells). RBC's are small disc-shaped bodies that contain hemoglobin, the iron-containing pigment that gives erythrocytes, or RBC's, their red color. Hemoglobin is a complex protein that carries oxygen from the lungs to the tissues. It then carries carbon dioxide, a waste product, from the tissues to the lungs to be expelled from the body.

There are approximately 4.5 to 6 million red blood cells per cubic millimeter of blood. This means that about 18 million RBC's are the size of a head of a pin. The appearance of erythrocytes, or RBC's, are referred to as biconcave because both sides of the red blood cell cave inward at the center. Having this shape allows RBC's to be flexible and pass through tiny capillaries. The average life span of a red blood cell is about 120 days.

4.) Leukocytes Maturation (White Blood Cells)

The second cellular portion consists of leukocytes, or WBC's (white blood cells). White blood cells fight infection. They protect the body against invasion of bacteria and other foreign material. WBC's leave the bloodstream and search for foreign material such as bacteria, viruses and toxins. Then they ingest and digest the foreign material. This process is called phagocytosis.

The average adult has between 5,000 and 10,000 WBC's per cubic millimeter of blood, unless an infection is present, in which case the number increases to fight the infection. Neutrophils are the most numerous of all the white cells, as well as being the main fighters against bacteria.

The various classifications of leukocytes are listed in Table 3.1 below.

Table 3.1 Leukocytes Classifications

Leukocytes	Function
Granulocytes	
Basophils	Least numerous type of leukocyte that releases histamine and heparin to damaged tissues
Eosinophils	Aids the body in fighting parasites which occurs in increased number in patients with allergies.
Neutrophils	Most numerous of the leukocyte which surrounds and digests pathogens found in tissue
Agranulocytes	
Monocytes	Large leukocyte formed in bone marrow that ingests bacteria, old red blood cells, and debris in tissues.
Lymphocytes	Leukocyte that multiplies in the lymphoid tissue and has a role in the body's immune system.

5.) Thrombocyte Maturation (Platelets)

The smallest of the formed blood elements are called platelets, or thrombocytes. Platelets are small fragments of special cells involved in coagulation. They have a round or oval disc shape, or plate-like appearance. They are half the size of erythrocytes and have a life span of 9 to 12 days while aiding in the clotting process. Platelets clump into small clusters when blood is shed. They release thrombokinase, which in the presence of calcium, reacts with prothrombin to produce thrombin. Thrombin converts to fibrin which then becomes the mesh-like blood clot.

When an injury occurs, platelets are the first cells to arrive at the site. Bleeding is diminished or stopped as a result of platelets sticking to the site of the injury and forming a platelet plug, which decreases blood flow from the injured site. Platelets are essential for minimizing blood loss as a result of an injury.

Chapter 3 – Review Questions

MULTIPLE CHOICE:

Select the best response for each of the following questions.

1. _________________ is a condition in which the skin turns a bluish color caused by lack of oxygen to the blood.

   i. basophils | j. anemia
   k. hyperkalemia | l. cyanosis

2. _________________ is an increase in the number of white blood cells.

   i. hypokalemia | j. leukocytosis
   k. hemophilia | l. phagocytosis

WORD SCRAMBLE:

Unscramble the word to fill in the blank:

3. **guoaailantcnt**

   _________________ is a substance that delays or prevents blood from clotting.

4. **orata**

   The _________________ is the largest artery in the body.

5. **hemoglobin**

   _________________ is a complex protein that carries oxygen from the lungs to the tissues.

6. **nuarmopyl**

   _________________ refers to the lungs and lung tissue.

TRUE OR FALSE:

Indicate if the following statements are true or false.

7. _______ There are two chambers in the heart, the atrial and the septa.
8. _______ Anemia is the deficiency of red blood cells, hemoglobin, or both.
9. Arteries carry oxyqenated blood away from the heart, and veins carry deoxygenated blood toward the heart.

FILL IN THE BLANKS:

Write the word(s) or statement needed to answer the following question:

10. Name the 3 types of blood cell:

____

____

____

chapter 4

Equipment and Supplies Used in Phlebotomy

Objectives

After completing this chapter, students should be able to:

- Identify equipment used in phlebotomy
- Identify proper use of syringes in specimen collection
- Identify proper use of needle gauges and evacuated system
- Identify proper use of additives and anticoagulants
- Recognize the 1.9 ratio of anticoagulant to blood
- Define hemoconcentration
- Recognize proper use of microcollection equipment
- Define Metric Terms and Metric System

Glossary Terms

Antiseptic	Germicidal solution used to clean the skin prior to venipuncture or dermal puncture.
Bevel	Point of a needle which has been cut at a slant for ease of entry.
Capillary Action	Process in which blood automatically flows into a thin tube.
Centrifuge	A piece of laboratory equipment that spins test tubes at a high speed and separates the cellular and liquid portions of the blood.
Evacuated Collection Tube	A glass or plastic tube with a stopper which contains a premeasured vacuum used for collecting blood.
Evacuated Tube Holder	A specialized plastic adapter which holds both a needle and a tube for blood collection; also referred to as an adapter or barrel.
Gauge	A unit of measure used to determine the dimension of a needle.
Liter	A metric fluid measure of 1000 milliliters; approximately 2 pints.
Milliliter	/1000 of a liter.
Requisition	A form used to order a blood test, usually generated by the physician.
Syringe	A device consisting of a plunger and a barrel.
Tourniquet	A device that stops the flow of blood.
Winged Infusion Set	A stainless steel collection needle connected to 5 to 12 inches of plastic tubing; also referred to as a butterfly needle set.

a. Equipment and Supplies

During the blood collection process, as well as during the transport of blood specimens, many different types of supplies and safety equipment are used by phlebotomists. They are listed below, along with descriptions and examples.

1.) Syringes and Needles

Needles are an important part of the blood collection process. A needle is composed of a hub, a shaft, and a bevel, or slanted tip at the point. Sterile needles, which are available in peel-apart packages or plastic cases, come in a variety of sizes by length and gauge. It is important to check the tip of the needle for damage, or blurs, including any small imperfections or rough edges, which can be painful to a patient. If a damaged needle is found, discard it in a sharps container and obtain a new one.

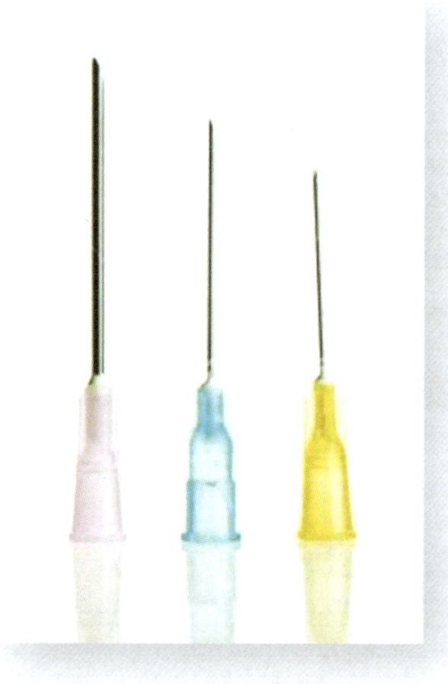

Figure 4.1 Needles in different sizes

2.) Needle Size and Gauges of Needles

Needles vary in size, from ¾ to ½ inches. The gauge of the needle, which refers to the size of its opening, also varies in size. This ranges from 16-gauge needles which are used to collect units of blood, to 23-gauge needles used for very small veins. The larger the gauge number, the smaller the opening of the needle. Routine venipuncture needles are usually 21 to 23 gauge and 1-inch long.

Needle adapters, or holders also come in a variety of sizes to accommodate different sizes of collection tubes.

3.) Types of Needles

Phlebotomists normally use three types of needles: A multiple-sample needle, used as part of an evacuated collection system (contains a double-pointed needle and a collection tube which contains a vacuum) A hypodermic needle, used with a syringe A butterfly (wing-tipped) needle

4.) Safety Syringes

At one time, syringes were the only option for blood collection. Use of syringes is no longer routine due to the use of the evacuated tube system (discussed later in this chapter). However, some patient's veins are too fragile for vacuum tubes during blood collection. In this case, safety syringes are used. Syringes are hazardous and can cause an increase in needlestick injuries. Therefore, proper care should be used when handling syringes.

For special specimen collection, 5 to 20 mL syringes are commonly used. It is important to make sure that the syringe is the correct size for the amount of blood to be collected.

5.) Butterfly Collection System

The butterfly needle, also called the winged infusion set, is commonly used when veins are very small or fragile, such as for elderly persons or children. On one end, it is a stainless steel beveled needle and tube with attached plastic wings. The plastic wings are used to hold the needle during insertion into the vein. On the other end, it has a luer fitting attached to it. The most common butterfly needle sizes are 21 and 23 gauge. The length of these needles range from ½ to ¾ inches long.

Use of butterfly needles can sometimes cause needlestick injuries because the needles have a tendency for one end to swirl and stick the individual who is disposing of the needle. To reduce butterfly needlestick injuries:

- Limit the use of butterfly needles except in the case where veins are difficult to access with a straight needle.
- Always use a safety-engineering butterfly needle.
- Be sure to stretch out the tubing when removing it from the package.
- Stabilize both ends of the tubing by holding both the plastic needle support and the syringe when disposing.
- Replace disposal containers as often as needed to make sure all needles can be disposed of properly.

6.) Sharps Containers

These are special containers used to dispose of needles and other sharp objects. They come in a variety of shapes and sizes. Be sure to dispose of needles in sharps containers immediately after use. Never open or tamper with a needle disposal container.

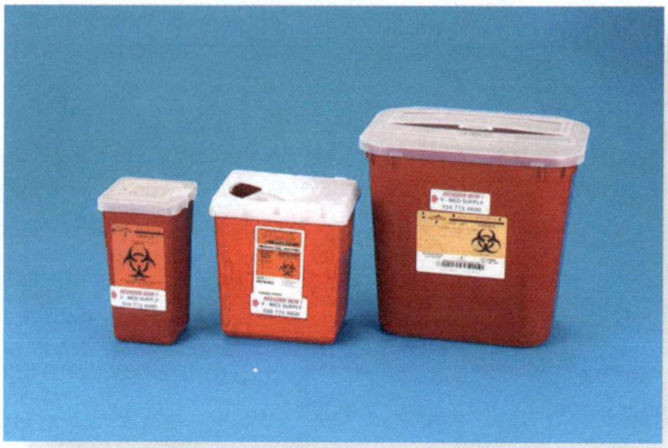

Figure 4.2 Sharps containers

7.) Tourniquets

A tourniquet is a length of rubber tubing that is wrapped around the arm during the blood collection process to temporarily stop the flow the venous blood. When a tourniquet is applied to the arm, the veins become enlarged. They are used during venipuncture to make it easier for the phlebotomist to locate the patient's veins.

The tourniquet should not be left on the arm longer than one minute, or hemoconcentration may occur. Hemoconcentration is a condition in which plasma enters the tissues, resulting in a higher than normal concentration of the cellular components of blood.

To prevent hemoconcentration:

1. Place the tourniquet on the patient's arm while you palpate the arm and select a vein.

2. Remove the tourniquet while you place gloves on and prepare equipment.

3. Reapply the tourniquet just prior to beginning the actual venipuncture.

As a rule of thumb, if it takes longer than a minute for blood collection, remove the tourniquet for at least one minute, then reapply the tourniquet.

8.) Gloves

Gloves may be latex or vinyl, and are available in a variety of sizes and styles. Vinyl gloves are normally used for individuals who are allergic to latex. Vinyl gloves are clear and latex gloves appear cloudy. Powered gloves are not recommended because powder can become a contaminant in or on the specimen.

OSHA requires that gloves be worn during the blood collection process and changed after each patient. Non-sterile gloves are acceptable during blood collection because the procedure is not a sterile procedure as in surgery. Remember to wash your hands after removing the gloves following venipuncture.

9.) Goggles

Safety goggles are now recommended when performing Phlebotomy procedures. Goggles are used to prevent the phlebotomist's eyes from being exposed to bloodborne pathogens from splashing or aerosol contaminants. Regular glasses are not a substitute for safety goggles.

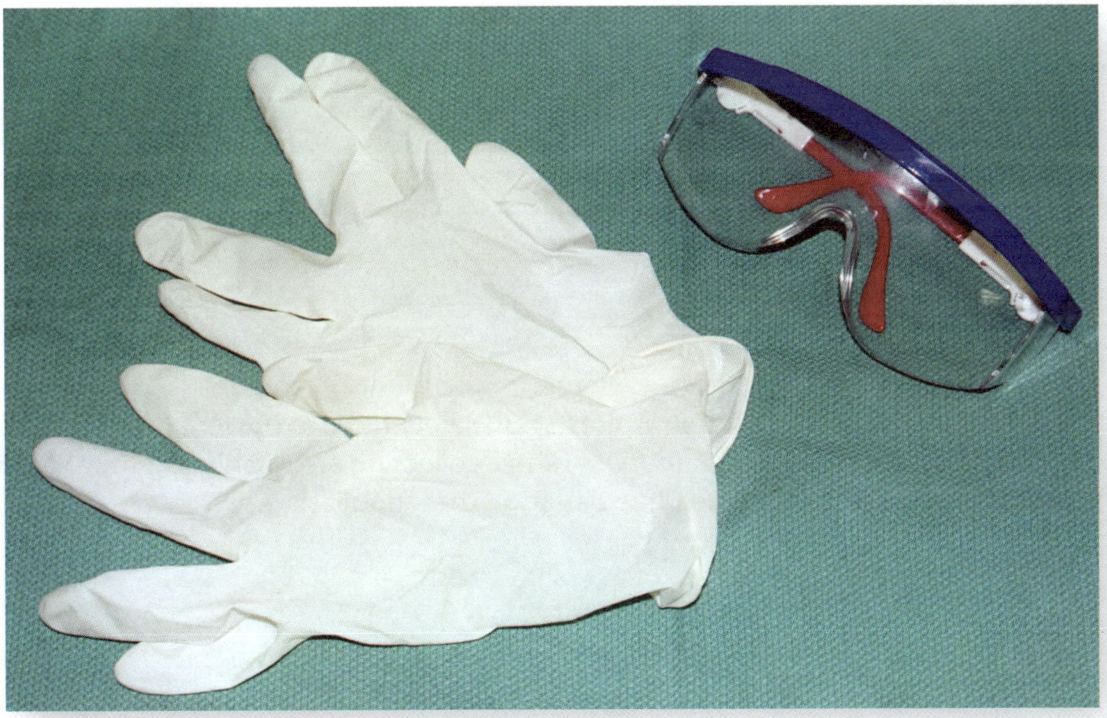

10.) Antiseptics, Gauge Pads and Bandages

Prior to performing venipuncture, the site must be properly cleaned using an antiseptic, such as a germicidal solution. Examples are alcohol prep pads, or sterile pads saturated with 70% isopropyl alcohol.

Alcohol prep pads are not recommended for the collection of blood alcohol levels, which requires additional sterility (in this case, iodine is used to clean the venipuncture site, or chlorhexiden gluconate as an alternative if the patient is allergic to iodine).

Immediately following withdrawal of the needle during venipuncture, a 2 x 2 inch gauze pad is applied with pressure to the site. Gauze can be folded and taped to the site which will maintain the proper amount of pressure to the site. A bandage can also be applied thereafter.

11.) Phlebotomy Chair

This special chair has adjustable armrests and safety locks to prevent falls in case of fainting. Generally found in outpatient blood-collecting areas, phlebotomy chairs may include storage areas for tubes, needles and other supplies.

12.) Microcollection Equipment

Rather than routine venipuncture, skin puncture blood-collecting equipment is normally used on infants. Using venipuncture on an infant is excessively hazardous. This is because the volume of blood to be collected from an infant is a lot less than that of an adult.

Lancets and Tubes - For infants, a penetration depth of less than 2.0 mm on heel sticks is recommended for blood collection, so as to avoid penetrating the infant's bone. This can be done through use of a skin puncturing device called a lancet.

Micro-containers - There are a variety of small specimen containers available including:

microcollection tubes – disposable plastic tubes which contain many of the same additives as evacuated tubes. capillary tubes – small, disposable glass or plastic tubes that fill by capillary action; also referred to as microhematocrit tubes, because they are centrifuged to determine the patient's hematocrit or packed cell volume. micropipettes – along with a dilution system, is a two-part system that collects the blood sample and stores it in a viral of diluting fluid for future testing.

13.) Specimen Collection Tray

It is important for all phlebotomists to have a well-equipped, organized blood collection tray for successful blood collection. The tray should be checked frequently and be kept clean at all times. It should be decontaminated with 10% bleach solution.

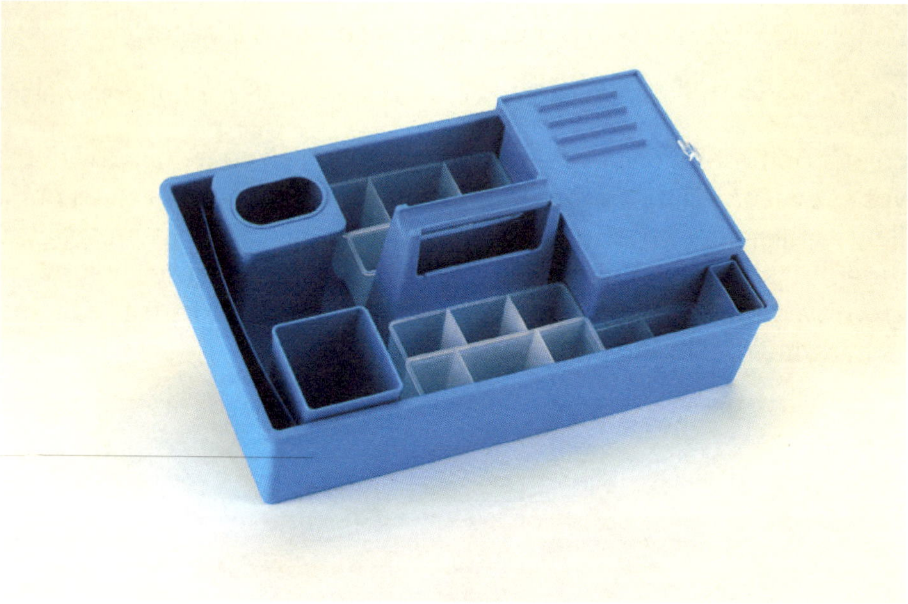

Figure 4.3 Blood Collection Tray

Supplies included in the blood or specimen collection tray:

- Disposable gloves
- Packaged alcohol wipes
- Chlorhexidine gluconate/alcohol pads
- Blood culture prep kits
- Gauze sponges (2 X 2)
- Permanent ink marker or marking pen
- Adhesive bandages Safety needles devices, needle holders, sterile needles, and butterfly needles
- Blood collection tubes
- Glass slides Micro-collection tubes
- Capillary tubes
- Fresh capillary tube sealer
- Retractable blood lancet devices
- Sterile blood lancets
- Tourniquets
- Sterile syringes
- Puncture resistant sharps container

b. Venipuncture Supplies

During venipuncture, there are specific supplies needed. This includes vacuum tubes, safety-needle collection devices, a tourniquet, supplies to cleanse the puncture site, labeling supplies, gloves, and special trays for the transport of the blood specimens.

The most frequently used equipment when performing venipuncture is the evacuated tube system, which consists of:

- A double-pointed needle
- An adapter to hold the needle and the collection tube
- A variety of color-coded evacuated collection tubes.

c. The Evacuated Tube System

Using the evacuated tube system, you can collect multiple tubes with a single venipuncture. It's a closed system which means the patient's blood flows from the vein through the needle and into the collection tube without exposure to air.

1.) Tube Make-up and Sizes

The tubes used in the evacuated tube system are made of glass or plastic and range in size from 2 to 15 milliliters (mL). Glass is not desirable because of the risk of exposure to bloodborne pathogens in the event of breakage.

The evacuated tubes fill automatically to a determined volume based on the amount of vacuum which is present inside the tube. They are color-coded based on the contents. In addition, a label is used to indicate the type of additive contained in the tube (either an anticoagulant or a clot activator), the draw volume and the expiration date. The expiration date refers to the last date that the tube can be used for blood collection. Most plastic collection tubes have a shorter expiration date than glass collection tubes.

Evacuated tubes are sterile and are sometimes coated with silicone, which prevents blood cells from sticking to the tube wall and stopper.

Evacuated tube holders are plastic adapters which hold both the needle and the tube for collection. They can be reused; however, once contaminated, they should be disposed of. Some newer safety needles have evacuated tube holders permanently attached. The whole assembly is then disposed of in one piece. Evacuated tube holders come in two sizes, for an adult-size collection tube and for a pediatric-size tube.

2.) Mechanism of Rubber Stopper

The rubber stopper of an evacuated tube is used to protect the vacuum inside. A vacuum is a space from which the air has been removed.

3.) Additives

In Phlebotomy, it is very important that the correct blood tube with the proper additive be used in blood collection; otherwise, the blood sample may be worthless.

Tubes with anticoagulants or clot activators are referred to as additive tubes. Anticoagulants are substances that prevent blood from clotting. They can be liquid or dry, and may be difficult to see in a tube.

Clot activators are substances that promote clotting. Examples of clot activators are glass, silica and thrombin).

4.) Important Tips to Remember

The vacuum in a collection tube allows the correct amount of blood to enter the tube. Do not underfill or overfill additive tubes because this can result in erroneous test results. Never transfer blood from one collection tube to another.

If your institution is located in a high altitude, this can decrease the vacuum in the tube. In this case, be extra careful to assure that tubes are filled properly. If needed, consult with your supervisor.

Blood collected in tubes containing an additive must be mixed promptly and thoroughly. Do not shake the tube. Mix by gently inverting the tube 5 to 10 times so that the additive is thoroughly mixed with the blood. Exceptions to this rule: light blue top sodium citrate tubes should be inverted no more than 3 to 4 times; pearl white top EDTA tubes should be mixed 8 to 10 times. If mixing is not thorough, a partial clot may form which can seriously interfere with blood results.

d. Centrifugation Process

During the centrifugation process, the blood specimen is spun rapidly to separate the cells from the liquid portion of the blood.

- Tubes should be centrifuged with closures in place.
- The centrifuge should have a top that securely tightly in place.
- Centrifuges should be temperature controlled because they internally generate heat.
- Specimens should not be centrifuged more than once.

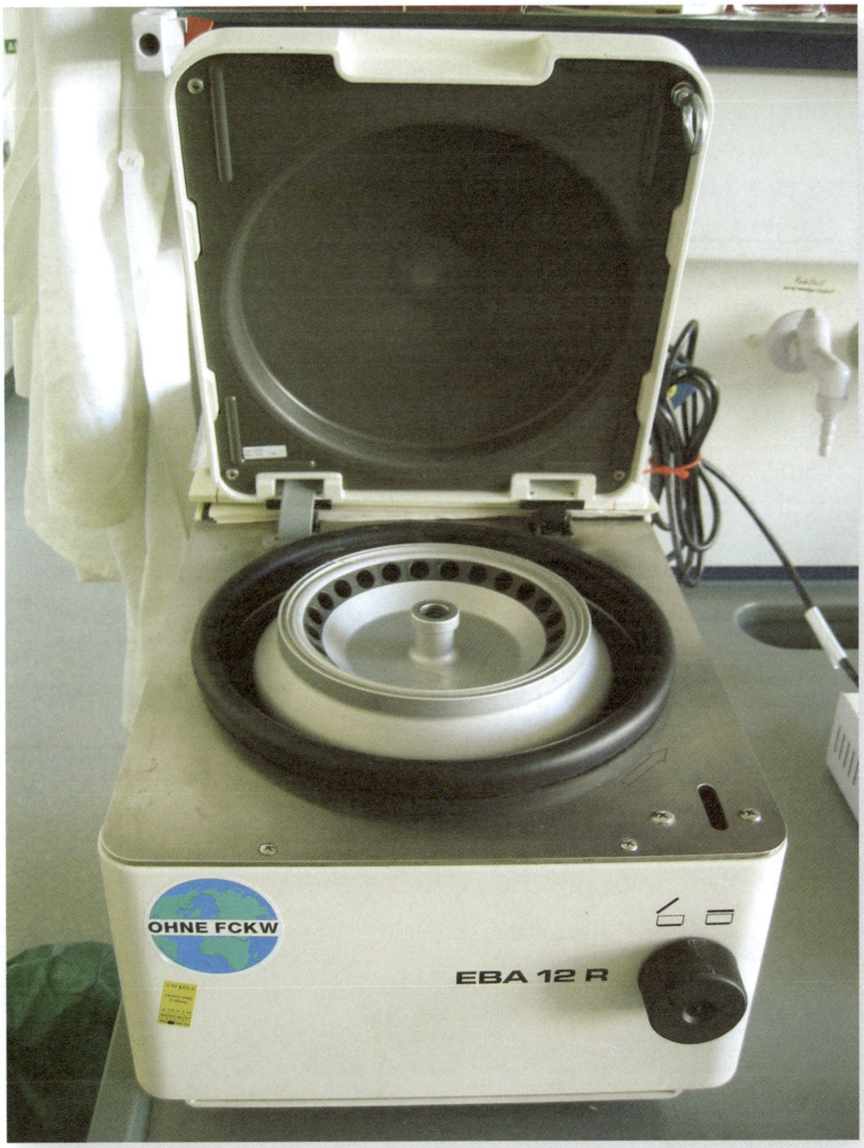

Figure 4.3 Examples of centrifuge equipment

e. Anticoagulants Used in Blood Collection Tubes

Anticoagulants are used to:

- Prevent coagulation of blood.
- Extend the life span and metabolism of the red blood cells after blood collection, since they often contain preservatives.
- Collect plasma for laboratory analysis.

Specific anticoagulants are needed depending on the test ordered.

The anticoagulants which are most frequently used are:

- **EDTA (ethylenediaminetetra-acetate)** – used primarily when performing blood cell counts (CBC). Additional applications include red cell folate, blood lead, hemoglobin A1c, and blood typing.
- **Sodium Citrate** – used primarily when performing studies such as prothrombin time.
- **Heparin** – used for a variety of routine and specialized tests. Different types of heparin may be used for different types of tests.
- **Fluordide-Oxalate** – used primarily for glucose and alcohol determinations. The fluoride inhibits enzymes, which may change glucose or alcohol concentrations; and the oxalate prevents clotting.

Additives such as oxalates, citrates, EDTA and heparin can prevent the coagulation of blood by removing calcium and forming insoluble calcium salts. Heparin is used in assays such as ammonia and plasma hemoglobin, and it prevents blood clotting by inactivating the blood-clotting chemicals, thrombin and factor X.

Whole Blood or Plasma Specimen – Non-Clotting

Using whole blood as a specimen decreases the time involved in acquiring the test result. This is because centrifugation is not required before laboratory testing.

f. Tubes and Anticoagulants

Color	Additive	Use	Test	Department
Lavender-Stoppered Tubes	Ethylenediaminetetra-acetate (EDTA)	Prevents blood from clotting by binding calcium; calcium is needed for clot formation	General hematological studies such as CBC, white cell (WBC) differential, platelet count and function tests	Hematology
Blue-Stoppered Tubes	Sodium Citrate	Like EDTA, sodium citrate is used to prevent coagulation by binding calcium	Prothrombin time (PT) and activated partial thromboplastin time (aPTT)	Hematology (Coagulation Section)
Green-Stoppered Tubes	Lithium Heparin, Sodium Heparin	Through use of heparin, which is a natural anticoagulant, it stops the coagulation process by inactivating thrombin and thromboplastin	Human leukocyte antigen (HLA) typing, chromosome analysis; assayed when plasma or whole blood is needed as in tests for ammonia	Chemistry
Gray-Stoppered Tubes	Sodium fluoride, Sodium fluoride with thymol, Potassium oxalate	Inhibits glycolytic action; when the ingredients in the left column are combined with potassium oxalate, clotting process is inhibited by binding calcium	Glucose analysis	Chemistry
Yellow-Stoppered Tubes	Sodium Polyanetholesulfonate	Protects the bacteria from the effects of the antibacterial properties of blood	Blood cultures	Microbiology
Red-Stoppered Tubes	No additive used	Used frequently for serology and chemistry tests and in blood bank for blood typing when both cells and serum are needed	Serum determinations	Chemistry and Serology
Tiger Tops and Gold Tubes	Clot activator and gel for serum separation	Special kind of speckled red-stoppered tube with a gold plastic cap over it called a splashguard, or Hemoguard, used to decrease aerosol mist which may be infectious	Serum determinations	Chemistry
Pink Tubes	Spray-dried EDTA	Used for whole blood hematology and immunohematology testing	Blood bank testing	Hematology
Royal Blue	No additive, or sodium heparin	Chemically cleaned to avoid any stray traces of materials	Toxicology studies, trace metal assays, nutritional analysis	Chemistry

g. Requisitions

The order for the blood test to be performed is generated by the physician and recorded on a requisition, either manually, or on a computer. The requisition must contain proper patient identification, including the patient's full name, room number (if an inpatient), unique patient number/medical record number and physician's name. In addition, the requisition should contain the date and time the test is to be performed, the type of test to be performed and the test status (timed, fasting, STAT, etc.).

It is the responsibility of the phlebotomist to examine all requisitions carefully prior to performing the blood collection. If there is missing information, the phlebotomist should obtain the missing information before proceeding to collect the specimen.

Paper Requisition Example:

LAB REQUEST/TEMPORARY REPORT **BLOOD TESTS** **PATIENT INFORMATION**

COMMENTS

SPECIAL INSTRUCTIONS PRINTED ON BACK OF FORM	Sect. Sig.
	Date for Collection
	Time for Collection AM PM
Time of Collection AM PM	Collected By

Patient Name
Patient Identification Number
Physician Name
Patient Location
Date of Birth

*Priority			HEMATOLOGY	RESULT
S	R	150	CBC	
S	R	187	CBC/Diff	
U	R	188	Retic 25-85 bill/L	
U	R	173	LE Prep Negative	
	R	162	Leukocyte Alk Phos	
	R	158	Sickle Cell Screen Neg.	
	R	152	ZSR 40-55%	
	R	170	Bone Marrow/Path	
	R	186	Hemogram/Path	
			SEROLOGY	
	R	606	ASO Sig.333	
	R	647	Candida Antigen Assay	
	R	608	Cold Agglutinin Sig. 1:32	
	R	663	CMV Ab. (Screen) Sig. 1:1	
	R	612	Cryptococcus Ag. Sig. 1:8	
	R	720	Febrile Aggl.	
	R	645	DNase B Titer	
	R	602	FTA-Abs	
	R	643	Fungal Immunodiffusion	
S	R	660	HCG-urine pregnancy	
	R	662	HIV-I Ab (HTLV III)	

*Priority			COAGULATION	RESULT
			PATIENT INFORMATION ☐ PATIENT RECEIVING HEPARIN ☐ PATIENT ON COUMADIN ☐ DRAWN FROM ARTERIAL LINE ☐ TO DETERMINE HEPARIN ACTIVITY ☐ TO DETERMINE COAG ACTIVITY W/O HEPARIN	
	R	32	Antithrombin 70-120%	
	R	48	Bleeding Time	
	R	30	Coag Screen	
S	R	108	DIC Screen	
U	R	106	D-Dimer <0.5 mg/L	
	R	18	Factor 8 Activity 50-150%	
	R	44	Factor 8 Antigen 50-150%	
	R	10	FSP <10ug/mL	
S	R	8	Fibrinogen	

*Priority			IMMUNOLOGY	RESULT
	R	377	AFP-nonpregnant	
	R	354	ANA <1:40	
	R	337	Anti-thyroid/microsomal	
	R		B & T cells, specify source	
	R	324	C-3 complement	
	R	329	C-4 complement	
	R	361	CEA nonsmoker	
			smoker	
	R	384	Ceruloplasmin	
	R	338	CRP <0.8 mg/dL	
	R	356	dsDNA <1:10	
	R	380	ENA (RNP/SM)	
	R	382	Haptoglobin	
	R	372	HAV Screen	
			Anti-HAV (IgG, IgM)	
	R	388	HBV Screen	
	R	365	HBsAg	
	R	370	Anti-HGs (HBsAb)	
	R	369	Anti-HBc(HBcAb)	
	R	387	Hepatitis Screen	
	R	429	Helper/Suppressor Ratio	

Computer-Generated Requisition Example:

P 000000 0601 02/27 #15432 220 NEAL JONES LAVH M 00123456 JANE SMITH, M.D. CBC DIFF RETIC	#15432 JONES,N #15432 JONES,N	#15432 JONES, N #15432 JONES, N	P 000000 0601 02/27 #15432 220 NEAL JONES LAVH M 00123456 JANE SMITH, M.D. CBC DIFF RETIC RCL 2/4/02 9:30am Collected by Date Time

h. Metric Terms and Metric System

As part of basic laboratory skills, phlebotomists should be familiar with metric conversion. The chart below lists common metric measurements.

METRIC MEASUREMENTS

Approximate Equivalencies

One Ounce	=	approximately 28 grams
Three and one-half ounces	=	100 grams
Eight ounces	=	227 grams
One pound	=	454 grams

Metric Conversions

1 kilogram	=	2.2 pounds
454 grams	=	1 pound
30 milliliters	=	1 ounce
1,000 liters	=	1 kiloliter
1 milliliter	=	1 cc
1,000 milliliters	=	1 liter

Translation

1 gallon	=	3.79 liters
1 quart	=	0.95 liters (or 950 milliliters or approximately 1 liter)
1 pint	=	0.48 liters (or 480 milliliters or approximately 500 ml)
1 cup (8 fluid ounces)	=	0.24 liters (or 240 milliliters or approximately 250 ml)
1 tablespoon	=	15 milliliters
1 teaspoon	=	5 milliliters

Chapter 4 – Review Questions

MULTIPLE CHOICE:

Select the best response for each of the following questions.

1. A _________________ is a unit of measure used to determine the dimension of a needle.

   a. liter
   b. bevel
   c. milliliter
   d. gauge

2. A _________________ is a piece of laboratory equipment that spins test tubes at a high speed and separates the cellular and liquid portions of the blood.

   a. centrifuge
   b. evacuated tube
   c. micropipette
   d. vacuum tube system

WORD SCRAMBLE:

Unscramble the word to fill in the blank:

3. **ptintiseac**

   An _________________ is a germicidal solution used to clean the skin prior to venipuncture or dermal puncture.

4. **rtniuoutqe**

   A _________________ is a length of rubber tubing that is wrapped around the arm during the blood collection process to temporarily stop the flow the venous blood.

5. **rsaphs**

   A _________________ container is a special container used to dispose of needles and other pointed objects.

6. **lesovg**

   OSHA requires that _________________ be worn during the blood collection process and changed after each patient. .

TRUE OR FALSE:

Indicate if the following statements are true or false.

7. ________ A requisition is a form used to order a blood test generated by a registered nurse.

8. ________ 8. The butterfly needle, also called the winged infusion set, is commonly used when veins are very small or fragile, such as for elderly persons or children.

FILL IN THE BLANKS:

Write the word(s) or statement needed to answer the following questions:

9. Name two types of micro-containers:

____

____

10. 1List one function of anticoagulant:

____

Chapter 5

Performing the Venipuncture

Objectives

After completing this chapter, students should be able to:

- Properly prepare for venipuncture procedure
- Recognize proper procedure for patient identification
- Define specimen labeling
- Locate common venipuncture sites in the human body
- Define step-by-step procedures for venipuncture
- Locate veins in the feet and ankles
- Handle patient reactions to venipuncture
- Identify proper technique for drawing blood from an indwelling line
- Recognize equipment used for arterial puncture
- Define the Allen Test
- Identify four arterial sites for arterial puncture
- Identify proper handling of arterial blood

Glossary Terms

Aliquot	A portion of a patient specimen used for testing.
Basal State	Metabolic condition after 12 hours of fasting and lack of exercise.
Collapsed Vein	An abnormal withdrawal of the vessel walls, stopping blood flow.
Ecchymosos	Discoloration or bruising causing by leakage of blood underneath the skin.
Edema	A condition in which the body tissues contain an excessive amount of fluid, resulting in swelling
Edematous	Swollen with an excessive accumulation of fluid.
Fasting	Abstinence from all food and liquids, except for water, for a specified period of time.
Petechiae	Small red spots on the skin due to minor hemorrhage in underlying tissue.
Venipuncture	Procedure in which a sharp object is inserted into a vein for withdrawing blood or infusing medications.

a. Venipuncture

Venipuncture signifies that blood collection will be performed from a vein. Before performing a venipuncture, it is important to properly prepare for the procedure.

To prepare for a routine venipuncture:

- Obtain and analyze the requisition slip.
- Decontaminate hands. Introduce yourself to the patient.
- Talk quietly and speak in a pleasant manner.
- Identify the patient.
- Position the patient comfortably.
- Explain the procedure you are about to perform.
- Verify diet restrictions and instructions to follow.
- Put on gloves.
- Prepare equipment and supplies.
- Select a venipuncture site.
- Apply a tourniquet.
- Cleanse the venipuncture site.
- Verify equipment and tube selection.

When performing a venipuncture:

- Collect samples in the appropriate tubes and in the correct order.
- Label the samples.
- Assess the patient to make sure bleeding has stopped.
- Decontaminate hands.
- Complete required documentation when the procedure is completed.

All steps in the venipuncture process are described in detail in the sections below.

b. Approaching the Patient

Social

When approaching the patient:

1. Introduce yourself.
2. Identify the patient (this is covered in more detail in the next section).
3. Gain the patient's confidence by explaining what you are about to do.
4. Reassure the patient and try to relieve any stress or tension which they may be experiencing.

Consider language such as "Good Morning. My name is I'm from the laboratory, and I'm here to collect a blood specimen for laboratory tests which your doctor has ordered." Telling the patient that the doctor has ordered tests emphasizes the importance of the patient care.

Avoid questions such as "How are you?" which may prompt the patient to explain their illness and reason for being there.

To respect patient confidentiality and in accordance with HIPAA regulations, do not verbalize the test(s) which have been ordered by the doctor.

Clerical

With regards to any information to be collected, be sure to review:

- Diet restrictions or check for allergies to latex.
- Instructions or procedures to be followed.

After information is collected, record any required documentation on all necessary forms and/or on the computer.

If the patient has not followed the requirements for fasting defined for the tests ordered, refer to the Standard Operating Procedure (SOP) or contact your supervisor for further assistance.

Technical

If any tools or equipment are needed, be sure to prepare any necessary equipment.

Patient Identification

One of the most important parts of the venipuncture procedure is proper patient identification. It is absolutely mandatory that the blood specimen be obtained from the correct patient.

If blood is collected from the wrong patient, this can pose a serious consequence to the phlebotomist, as well as pose a critical medical risk to the patient.

Patient Identification Procedure

Always ask the patient their full name. Never ask "Are you Mr. Jones?" Patients often answer "Yes" to questions, even when they are not certain what was asked.

If the patient is wearing a wristband, check the following information:

- Hospital or Medical Record Number
- Name of Patient
- Name of Doctor

Compare the full name which the patient has given you with the full name on the wristband (if on-hand), as well as the full name of the requisition.

If the patient is a small child or infant, consult with a relative or family member to identify the patient by name, address, or birth date; then, verify the information on the requisition.

If the patient cannot be identified, do not perform the phlebotomy.

An aliquot is a portion of a patient specimen used for testing. Once the specimen is divided into smaller portions, or aliquots, simultaneous testing in different laboratory areas can be accomplished. The separated specimens are then placed in separate containers. Therefore, correct patient identification of specimens is critical.

c. Accessioning Order

General Procedure

Blood collection should never be drawn without a physician's order, or requisition. Requisitions vary from one health care institution to another, including use of a paper requisition, or computerized requisition. The advantage of a computer-generated requisition is that it is often accompanied by a pre-printed patient label which can be placed on the tube after blood collection.

Most requisitions contain the same basic information including:

- Patient's name
- Patient's unique identification number
- Patient's location
- Name(s) of test(s) ordered
- Physician's name
- Date and time of specimen collection
- Patient diagnosis
- Patient date of birth
- Patient gender

Before proceeding with the blood collection, the phlebotomist should check the requisition carefully to make sure all necessary equipment for the ordered tests is on-hand.

Emergency Room

When a phlebotomist is performing venipuncture in an Emergency Room, the following problems may exist:

- The patient may be unconscious
- The patient may not have an identification band
- The identity of the patient may be unknown
- The working environment may be a lot busier and disorganized as compared to a laboratory

Phlebotomists should be prepared to perform their duties quickly and accurately in a variety of environments, including areas which may be more hectic and stressful, such as an Emergency Room.

d. American Association for Blood Banks Standards for Labeling of Blood Bank Specimens

The AABB (American Association of Blood Banks) provides standards of care followed by physicians, nurses and phlebotomists when caring for patients. Approximately 2,000 institutions, including community and hospital blood banks, hospital transfusion services and laboratories, and about 8,000 individuals, including physicians, nurses and other health care providers; scientists; administrators; medical technologists; blood donor recruiters; and public relations practitioners, are members of AABB. AABB's active members are located in all 50 states and 80 countries.

AABB Code of Ethics and Bylaws:

http://www.aabb.org/Documents/Join_AABB/ethicsbylaws.pdf

To access information about specimen labeling, go to http://www.aabb.org, select *Members Area*, then select *Labeling*. Membership is required.

Source: The AABB website, http://www.aabb.org

Positioning the Patient

When positioning a patient for venipuncture, be sure that:

- The vein used for blood collection is easily accessible.
- The patient is comfortable in the phlebotomy chair (or hospital bed or chair if he/she is an inpatient).
- The patient's arm is supported by a firm surface, such as an armrest on a phlebotomy chair or on the bed if the patient is lying down.
- The patient will not fall if they have a reaction by making sure there is adequate support for the arm.

Remember to:

- Never place an equipment tray on a patient's bed or chair arm.
- Never label tubes prior to collection.
- Never leave equipment in the room.

e. Applying the Tourniquet

Once the patient's arm is in a comfortable position, place the tourniquet firmly around the upper arm. The tourniquet makes it easier to feel, or palpate the vein for the venipuncture. The most common location to perform a venipuncture is in the anecubital area of the arm, so the tourniquet should be placed approximately 3 to 4 inches above the elbow. Be sure the tourniquet is tight enough to increase blood pressure in the veins, but not too tight that it cuts off the circulation. Do not leave the tourniquet on the patient for more than 1 minute, otherwise, hemoconcentration will occur. Hemoconcentration is a condition in which plasma enters the tissues, resulting in higher than normal concentration of the cellular components of blood.

f. Selecting the Appropriate Venipuncture Site

As discussed and shown in chapter 3, the median cubital vein is the preferred vein when performing venipuncture. The cephalic vein is not preferred as it has a tendency to roll. The basilic vein should be avoided because it lies close to the brachial nerve and artery.

In selecting the appropriate venipuncture site, follow the steps below:

1. Prior to performing the venipuncture, be sure to wash your hands and then put on new, properly fitting, sterile gloves. It is recommended that you consults your institution's policy and procedure and follow proper guidelines.

2. Attach a sterile, unused needle to the needle holder and assemble the necessary blood collection tubes. Be sure to have extra blood collection tubes handy in case problems occur with the original tubes. Some phlebotomists may choose to do this prior to applying the tourniquet, which is preferable.

3. As discussed in the previous section, remember to not leave the tourniquet on for more than 1 minute while you search for a vein. If 1 minutes passes, remove the tourniquet for at least 3 minutes before re-applying it on the patient.

4. Inspect and palpate the area to find a vein, even if the vein can be seen. The vein will feel like an elastic tube that gives if you apply pressure with your finger. Arteries pulsate, so be sure that the structure you feel is not pulsating.

5. If a vein has been used repeatedly for fluid injections or punctures, it may feel cord-like. If this is the case, do not use that vein because it may be difficult to obtain blood from it.

6. If you are having trouble locating a vein, try massaging the arm from wrist to elbow. This will force blood into a vein. Alternatively, you can try tapping sharply with the index and second finger 2 or 3 times, which may cause the vein to dilate.

7. If necessary, place a warm, damp washcloth on the skin for a few minutes to make the veins stand out.

8. If you aren't sure if you have located a vein, try inspecting the patient's other arm. In some cases, veins are small in one arm, and large in the other arm.

9. Venipuncture should be avoided in any areas which are edematous, or full of swelling. Edema occurs when excessive fluid collects in the tissues of the patient, causing swelling. Blood should not be drawn from areas with edema because it may be difficult to locate a vein, and the specimen may be diluted with tissue fluid, which can adversely affect the results of blood tests.

10. Also, venipuncture should not be performed on an area that has a hemotoma, which is a bruise from a previous venipuncture. Additionally, venipuncture should not be performed in areas with lymphostatis, or lack of fluid drainage in the lymph system. Lymphostatis commonly occurs in patients who have had lymph nodes removed.

g. Performing a Safe Venipuncture

1. Prior to performing the venipuncture, cleanse the site with 70% isopropyl alcohol by making outward concentric circles. Allow the area to dry, or wipe dry using a gauge pad. Do not blow on the site, as this can contaminate the area. Also, do not touch the site; if touched, the site must be re-cleansed.

2. During the puncture, the vein should be fixed, or held taut. To do this:

    - Place your thumb about an inch below where the needle is to enter and press down on the arm; and,
    - At the same time, pull the skin towards the hand. The fingers of your hand should be around and underneath the patient's arm, grasping the patient's arm as your thumb stretches and holds the vein taut. Do not straddle the site with a thumb and finger which may increase the chances of inadvertently sticking yourself.

3. Before inserting the needle:

    - Be sure that the needle is in line with the vein.
    - Be sure that the needle is at approximately a 15-degree angle with the skin.
    - Remove the cap and inspect the needle. If any nicks or burrs or found, discard the needle and blood tube holder in an approved puncture-resistant sharps container.

4. Insert the first tube into the evacuated tube holder resting on the inside needle. Do not push all the way down because this will cause the vacuum seal of the tube to break. In certain cases, you may choose to use a butterfly wing set rather than an evacuated tube collection system.
5. Inform the patient that the venipuncture is about to occur. Ask the patient to keep his or her arm still during the venipuncture.
6. Introduce the needle with the bevel up. The bevel is the flattened area that extends back from the tip.
7. Grip the holder firmly and keep it steady when introducing the needle. Do not hesitate to assure that the puncture is performed with a clean, smooth motion.
8. Note that a little give will occur as the needle enters the vein.
9. After the vein is punctured, decrease the angle of the needle and slide the needle further into the vein.
10. When the needle is in the vein, push the collection tube all the way down into the blood tube holder, keeping the needle as stable as possible. Blood should then flow into the tube due to the vacuum in the tube.
11. As blood flows into the collection tube, watch the flow until completion and the tube has been filled.
12. As soon as the tube is filled, hold the blood tube holder steady and carefully pull the tube out without dislodging the needle from the vein. If the tube contains an additive, mix the contents by gently inverting it 5 to 10 times before the next tube is inserted into the blood tube holder. Exceptions: light blue top sodium citrate tubes should be inverted no more than 3 to 4 times; pearl white top EDTA tubes should be mixed 8 to 10 times.
13. If additional tubes are needed, slide the next tube in and press firmly so that the stopper is fully penetrated by the needle.
14. Remove the last collection tube from the holder before removing the needle from the vein.
15. If blood collection requires several minutes, remove the tourniquet as soon as there is good blood flow into the tube.
16. Remove the tourniquet before withdrawing the needle from the puncture site.
17. After removing the needle from the puncture site, immediately discard the needle and blood tube holder into the approved puncture-resistant sharps container.

18. Apply clean gauge over the puncture site. Never use an alcohol pad to maintain pressure and stop the bleeding. Instruct the patient to apply pressure and keep his or her arm straight. If the patient is unable to do so, as a phlebotomist, it is your responsibility to apply pressure until the bleeding has stopped. Refer to your institution's policies and procedures, which may vary. For example, for outpatients, a bandage is sometimes used to cover the site after venipuncture.
19. Label the specimen (covered in more detail in the "Identification of the Specimen" section below).
20. Remove and discard you gloves; then, wash your hands before proceeding to the next patient.

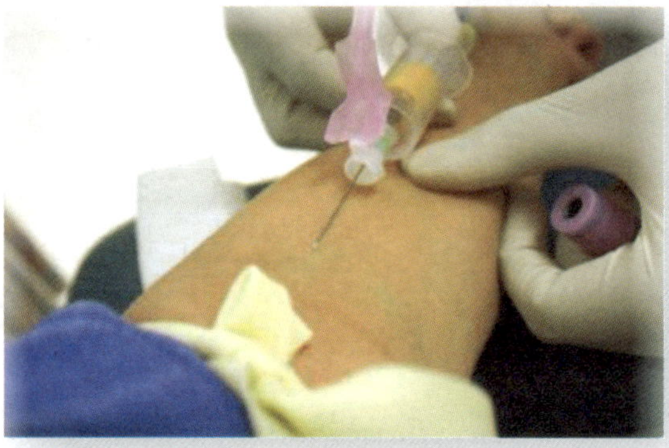

h. Order of Draw for Blood Collection Tubes

During venipuncture, additives may carry-over into other tubes and cause cross contamination. Also, skin surface bacteria may lead to incorrect blood results and tissue fluids may interfere with coagulation studies. In order to reduce the chance of errors as well as produce good blood results, it is important for the phlebotomist to fill collection tubes in the correct order.

The recommended order of draw is as follows:

1. Blood culture tubes with yellow tops
2. Empty tubes, with no additives, generally with red tops
3. Coagulation tubes with light blue tops
4. Heparin tubes, with green tops
5. EDTA tubes, with lavender or pink tops
6. Glycolytic inhibitor tubes, with gray tops
7. Trypsin inhibitor and bothrops attox venum, with royal blue tops

i. Syringe vs. Evacuated Tube Specimen Collection

Venipuncture by Syringe

Syringes are not widely used for venipuncture due to various safety concerns, including accidental cross-contamination of anticoagulants if the blood specimen is injected into multiple evacuated tubes using the same needle and syringe.

Use of a blood transfer device can minimize problems associated with using a syringe.

In infants, children, and some adults who have small veins, a butterfly needle set with a syringe can be used. If a smaller amount is needed (less than 10 ccs), a needle attached directly to a syringe may suffice. If a butterfly needle set is used with evacuated tubes, the small or delicate vein may collapse. Since the syringe does not have a vacuum, the amount of pressure applied to a small vein can easily be controlled. In this respect, use of the syringe vs. evacuated tube can be helpful.

Venipuncture by Evacuated Tube Method

CLSI (Clinical and Laboratory Standards Institute) recommends that venipuncture specimens be collected through a method which allows blood to flow directly into the tubes. Examples are the evacuated tube systems, and winged infusion systems.

Small evacuated collection tubes should be used with winged infusion sets to avoid fragile veins being collapsed.

The evacuated tube method should be used because:

- It is fast and relatively safe
- You can obtain the best specimen quality
- Large collection amounts are possible

The evacuated tube method should not be used with:

- Small veins
- Fragile veins
- Difficult draws
- Small children
- Hands or feet

j. Failed Venipuncture

Remember that positioning the needle properly is critical. If the tip of the needle is not inserted all the way in the vein, blood flow will be inadequate. In this case, lower the angle and advance the needle a little more. If the needle appears to have missed the vein, be sure that the vein is fixed using your thumb, and partially pull the needle back without removing it from the skin; then, attempt to puncture the vein again.

If the tube does not have sufficient vacuum, blood flow may be inadequate. In this case, try another tube before withdrawing the needle.

Do not attempt a venipuncture more than twice in one session. If you cannot obtain a blood sample, have another person attempt to draw, or perform a skin puncture if possible.

If blood is drawn too quickly or forcefully during venipuncture, this can result in a collapsed vein. A collapsed vein is more common when blood is collected from smaller veins. For smaller veins, use a smaller blood collection tube and/or a smaller needle size. If problems persist, consider using a syringe which can be used to control the force of the vacuum exerted on the vein.

k. Intravenous and Indwelling Lines

If the patient is receiving an intravenous infusion, it is preferable to use the other arm for venipuncture. In certain circumstances, it is possible to use the same arm which is receiving intravenous fluid. The blood may be collected from a vein which is several centimeters away, below the point of IV infusion, with the tourniquet placed in between. The IV may be stopped by nursing personnel.

If venipuncture is performed when IV infusion is present, be sure to document it on the test requisition. Record the IV fluid which is flowing. For example, "intravenous of 5% glucose running", or "blood transfusion".

Never draw blood from a vein above or just below the point where the patient is receiving an IV fluid infusion.

If the patient has a cannula, fiscula, or vascular graft in his or her arm, consult with a physician prior to blood collection. A cannula is a temporary surgical connection between an artery and a vein. A fiscula is an artificial connection between an artery and vein. Both of these may be found in patients who require a long-term dialysis or long-term IV medication.

I. Identification of the Specimen

After blood collection, label the specimen in the presence of the patient.

Never pre-label specimen tubes. If the pre-labeled specimen tube is left in your tray, it can mistakenly be used for another patient.

Specimen tubes should be labeled with:

- Patient's full name
- Patient ID number
- Institution ID (if needed)
- Date of collection
- Time of collection
- Phlebotomist ID/initials (if needed)

The identity of the phlebotomist must be documented on the test requisition. Check your institution's proper labeling procedures since policies may vary. In most cases, the phlebotomist's initials are noted on the requisition, specimen collection list, and/or the collection tube label. If the test performed was not routine, you may need to record the site of collection as well. Be sure to use a permanent marker and/or computer-generated label (if available).

The three reasons why it is necessary to label the specimen with the required information are:

1. Clerical error(s) must be prevented when identification of specimens collected.
2. It is important to know the identity of the phlebotomist in the event that he or she needs to be contacted for questions.
3. The exact time of the blood collection is needed to interpret results.

In addition, it is important to properly label specimens in the presence of the patient in order to:

1. Inspect the venipuncture site for hemostasis (cessation of bleeding) before leaving the patient; and,
2. Give the patient a feeling confidence as to what is being done with the specimen.

Be careful not to contaminate the test requisition or specimen collection list. If this occurs, they must be copied and discarded according to your institution's policies and procedures.

If specimens are to be mailed or transported via a commercial transportation company, they must be packaged and labeled properly.

m. Criteria for Recollection or Rejection of a Specimen

As a phlebotomist, it is important to be familiar with your institution's criteria for rejecting specimens. Since rejected specimens mean additional work for the phlebotomist, it is best to avoid collecting blood samples which will be rejected by the laboratory.

The following are reasons why specimens may be rejected:

- Incorrect or irregular specimen labeling
- Hemolyzed specimen
- Incorrect tube used
- Partially filled tube
- Improper handling of specimen
- Improperly mixed tube
- Expired tube used
- Incorrect collection time

n. Prioritizing Specimen Collection

In addition to properly preparing the patient for blood collection, it is critical that the timing of the collection also be accurate. Laboratory requisitions normally note the time which the blood sample should be drawn. As a phlebotomist, it is important to recognize that certain types of tests, such as glucose tolerance tests, require blood collection to be completed at a certain time of day. When a stat laboratory requisition is received, the phlebotomist must draw the blood immediately and quickly deliver the specimen to the laboratory.

Timed specimens may be prioritized as:

- **Stat** – must be done immediately; results must be known as soon as possible in order to treat a critically ill patient.
- **Timed** – to be done at a particular time of day
- **Lipenic** – for fasting tests

For more information on timed specimens, see Chapter 9, Special Specimen Collection.

o. Arterial Punctures

Arterial punctures are performed to test arterial blood gases (ABG's). They measure the ability of the lungs to exchange oxygen and carbon dioxide. In order to assess blood gases, arterial blood is needed. Generally, a nurse or respiratory therapist with special training will collect arterial blood to be evaluated for blood gases such as O2, CO2, and pH. Arterial puncture training must include:

- Complications associated with arterial puncture
- Precautions for patient safety
- Specimen handling procedures

Not all arteries can be used to perform an arterial puncture. Common arteries used are:

- Umbilical Artery
- Femoral Artery
- Brachial Artery
- Radial Artery

p. Allen Test

Before performing an arterial puncture on the radial artery, an Allen test must be performed. An Allen test is used to determine if an artery is safe to use for ABG (Arterial Blood Gas) test. It determines if there is collateral circulation and checks that both the ulnar artery and the radial artery are supplying blood to the area.

To perform an Allen test:

- Support the patient's wrist and have them make a fist.
- Using the second and third fingers of both hands, not including the thumb, occlude both the ulnar and the radial arteries.
- Have the patient slowly open his or her fist several times until the palm is pale. Release the pressure on the ulnar artery while keeping the radial artery occluded.
- If the ulnar artery is functioning properly, the color should return to the palm within 5 to 10 seconds. If the ulnar artery is not functioning properly, an arterial puncture should not be performed on the radial artery.

q. Arterial Puncture Procedure

The puncture site should be cleansed to prevent infection. The area should be wiped with a povidone-iodine (Betadine) solution. Do not use alcohol swabs because the alcohol may interfere with the blood results.

No tourniquet is needed because the existing pressure in the arteries.

A syringe may be used because only a small amount of blood is needed. Normally, an arterial sample is collected using a 1 to 5 mL syringe with a 21 to 23 gauge needle. The syringe is precoated with liquid lithium heparin to prevent the sample from clotting.

The skin is pulled taut and the syringe is held like a dart with the bevel of the needle facing up. The artery is pierced at a 45-degree angle for the radial artery and a 90-degree angle for the femoral artery. Blood should flow into the syringe through use of the pressure of the blood in the artery. There is no need to pull back on the plunger of the syringe.

As soon as collection is completed, the needle should be removed and pressure should immediately be applied to the site with sterile gauge. The syringe should be capped, placed in ice, and transported to the laboratory as soon as possible. This is needed to preserve the integrity of the specimen. The test should be performed within 10 minutes of the blood collection.

The phlebotomist, or person performing the arterial puncture, should apply pressure on the site for at least 15 minutes after collection. This is because it takes much longer for bleeding to stop in artery than in a vein. Never allow the patient to maintain pressure. Be sure to inform the nurse that an arterial puncture was performed so that he or she can assess the puncture site periodically.

In addition, the phlebotomist, or person performing the procedure, should check for a pulse below the site of the puncture. If the pulse is absent, notify the nurse at once.

Chapter 5 – Review Questions

MULTIPLE CHOICE:

Select the best response for each of the following questions.

1. _________________ is a condition in which the body tissues contain an excessive amount of fluid, resulting in swelling.

   m. ecchymosos
   n. petechiae
   o. lymphostatis
   p. edema

2. When positioning a patient for venipuncture, remember to:

   e. Never place an equipment tray on a patient's bed or chair arm.
   f. Never label tubes prior to collection.
   g. Never leave equipment in the room.
   h. All of the above.

WORD SCRAMBLE:

Unscramble the word to fill in the blank:

3. **qalotiu**

   _________________ is a portion of a patient specimen used for testing.

4. **uctipvurenne**

   _________________ is a procedure in which a sharp object is inserted into a vein for withdrawing blood or infusing medications.

TRUE OR FALSE:

Indicate if the following statements are true or false.

5. _______ Syringes are widely used for venipuncture.
6. _______ The evacuated tube method should be used in venipuncture because it is fast and relatively safe, you can obtain the best specimen quality, and large collection amounts are possible.
7. _______ It is okay to pre-label specimen tubes.

FILL IN THE BLANKS:

Write the word(s) or statement needed to answer the following questions:

8. What information should be checked on a patient wristband to correctly identify the patient? (Name three items):

 ____

 ____

 ____

9. What should you do if you if the test requisition or specimen collection list becomes contaminated?

 ____

 ____

 ____

10. List at least 3 reasons why specimens may be rejected:

 ____

 ____

 ____

Chapter 6

Dermal Capillary Puncture

Objectives

After completing this chapter, students should be able to:

- Identify when to perform a dermal puncture
- Define lancets
- Recognize proper use of microcollection equipment
- Identify steps for dermal puncture procedure

Glossary Terms

Calcaneus	Heel bone.
Geriatric	Pertaining to the elderly.
Hematocrit	A blood test used to help detect anemia.
Interstitial	Space between cells and tissue.
Osteomyelitis	Infection of inflammation of the bone or bone marrow.
Palmar	Palm side of the hand.
Plantar	Sole side of the foot.

a. When to Perform a Dermal Puncture

Although venipuncture is the most frequently performed phlebotomy procedure, there may be times then it isn't suitable, such as in small children, or in cases where no adequate veins are available. In this case, a shallow puncture of the skin is made, usually on the patient's fingers or heels, to obtain a small amount of blood for testing. A dermal puncture specimen is composed of interstitial fluid, which is a mixture of fluid found between cells and tissues, and a small amount of blood from capillaries, venules and arterioles.

Perform a dermal puncture rather than a venipuncture if:

- The patient is an infant or small child
- Tests only require a few drops of blood
- The patient is very apprehensive about a venipuncture procedure
- The patient has severe burns
- The patient's veins must be reserved for therapeutic purposes, such as IV lines
- The patient has fragile veins
- Frequent blood sampling is needed (every 1 to 2 hours for example)

Dermal Puncture should not be performed when:

- The patient is severely dehydrated
- The patient is in shock
- The patient has poor circulation
- The patient is extremely cold
- Not enough blood can be obtained for all tests ordered via a skin puncture
- Blood bank or blood culture tests are ordered

b. Selecting a Site for Dermal Puncture

When selecting a dermal puncture, select a site that is warm and pink rather than cold and blue.

Warming the site of the dermal puncture increases blood flow; thereby making the collection process easier and reducing the amount of tissue fluid collected.

Two main sites used for dermal puncture are:

- Third or fourth fingertip
- Heel (if under age 1)

Occasionally, the sole-side (plantar) surface of the big toe or the earlobe is used as a dermal puncture site.

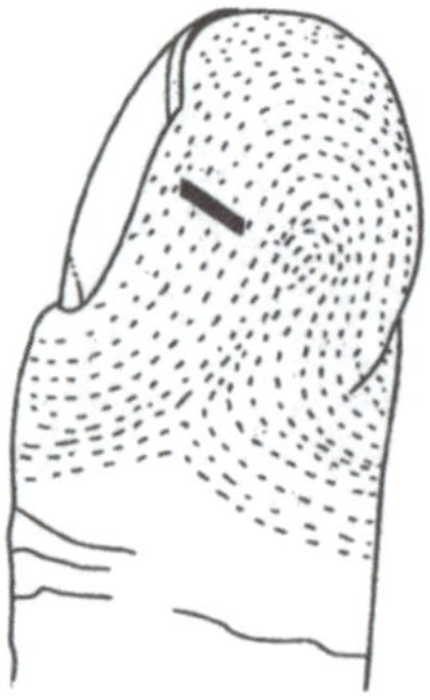

Puncture Site on Finger

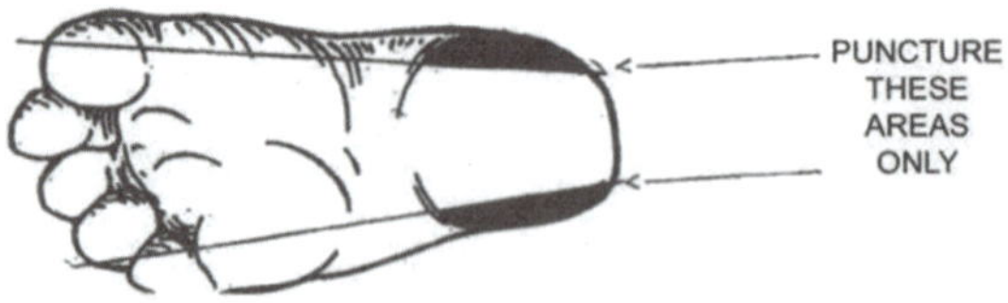

Infant heel: The darkened areas illustrate the acceptable areas for puncture. The little toe side is the primary area of choice.

Printed with permission from Magic Valley Regional Medical Center

c. Methods of Puncturing the Finger – Collecting Samples

There are a variety of micro-specimen containers available for micro-samples (samples of less than 1 milliliter). They are listed below

1.) Lancets

Lancets are the most simplest of the skin-puncturing devices. They are composed of a single-use, sterile, disposable metal blade that comes individually wrapped. Some lancets are all metal and come in individual foil pouches, while others are plastic and the sterile metal blade is exposed by twisting off a plastic cover.

Lancets are used to control the depth of the puncture when performing a dermal puncture.

2.) Spring-loaded Lancet

A spring-loaded skin-puncturing device that triggers an automatic release of the blade when pushed up against the skin; this produces an automatic puncture. With most devices, the blade retracts into the device after the incision is made.

The color of the spring-loaded lancet determines the depth of the puncture made by the blade.

3.) Capillary Action

Capillary action is the physical process of blood flowing, or being pulled, into a very thin tube. It eliminates the needs to tip the tube downward which reduces the risk of getting air bubbles in the sample.

4.) Calibrated Micropipette

A micropipette is a very small pipette (small tube into which blood is drawn by suction) used in microcollection. It is frequently used for hematology tests on small blood samples. A micropipette with a dilution system consists of a calibrated capillary tube, which collects the blood sample, and a vial which stores the fluid for laboratory testing. The size of the capillary pipette may vary depending on the type of test ordered.

5.) Microhematocrit Capillary Tubes

Microhematocrit tubes are small plastic tubes or glass tubes wrapped in a thin Mylar filament. These wrapped tubes are used because of the increase breakage of capillary tubes in the past. They are commonly used when a hematocrit is requested. A hematocrit is a blood test used to help detect anemia.

6.) Red Tipped MicrocollectionTubes

Red-tipped microcollection tubes are coated with heparin on the inside to prevent clotting of the specimen. They are used to measure hematocrit.

7.) Microcontainer or Microvette

Microcontainers are microcollection containers which provide a larger collection volume than capillary tubes. Microcontainers come with a variety of anticoagulants, similar to the evacuated tube system. They also use the same type of color-coded system as used with evacuated tubes and are mixed the same way. Although microcontainers are smaller than evacuated tubes, proper mixing is just as important. Without proper mixing of the additive and specimen, the blood will clot; a clotted specimen cannot be use for laboratory testing. Centrifuging the microcollection tubes can be done to separate the cells from the serum or plasma.

Microvette-capillary blood collection is another microcollection system with a full range of anticoagulants and serum separation gel. The system can be used to collect, store, and separate samples in the same unbreakable, disposable container.

8.) Unopette System

A collection system used for hematology tests; used to make accurate dilutions of whole blood. The system consists of a sealed plastic reservoir containing a measured amount of fluid (the amount depends on the test ordered), a calibrated glass capillary pipette in a plastic holder, and a plastic pipette shield. Common procedures in which Unopette devices are used include WBC count, RBC count, platelet count, and RBC fragility.

9.) Specimen Collection Trays

The follows are items to include on Blood Microcollection Tray:

- 70% isopropyl alcohol and iodine or Betadine pads
- Permanent ink marker or marking pen
- Microcollection blood serum separator tubes
- Capillary whole blood cell collectors
- Safety lancets for skin puncture
- Sterile gauze pads or bandages
- Unheparinized plastic microcollection tubes
- Heparinized plastic microcollection tubes
- Heparinized Natelson tubes
- Unopette devices for collection and dilution procedures
- Disposable gloves
- Appropriate warming device
- Thermometer Glass microscope slides
- Capillary safety tube sealer
- Antimicrobial hand gel or foam to wash hands without soap and water
- Puncture resistant sharps container

d. Dermal Puncture Procedure

Follow these steps to perform a skin puncture:

1. Review requisition and check to see what tests were ordered.
2. Assemble any necessary equipment.
3. Wash your hands with either an alcohol-based hand rub (if hands are not visible soiled) or soap and water (if hands are visibly soiled).
4. Greet and identify the patient.
5. Put on new, properly fitting gloves.
6. Select the site for the dermal puncture, which will be one of the following:
    a. just off the center of the middle or ring finger of the non-dominant hand
    b. the lateral curved surface of the heel
    c. the heel of an infant
7. Warm the puncture site if necessary, by massaging the area to increase blood flow. Avoid a finger or other site which is cold, cyanotic (blue), swollen or inflamed.
8. Using both hands, grasp the finger or heel firmly with your non-dominant hand. Now cleanse the site with alcohol and wipe dry using clean gauze.
9. Select the proper size of a disposable lancet, based on the age and weight of the patient, as well as the volume of blood required.
10. Using the disposable lancet, make an incision.
11. Dispose of the lancet in a sharps container.

12. Wipe away the first drop of blood, which may be contaminated with tissue fluid, or residue from your alcohol wipe.
13. Apply pressure to the site.
14. Collect the specimen in capillary tubes or microcollection containers. Be sure to avoid air bubbles by keeping the capillary tube opening in the blood and not exposed to the air.
15. Apply clean gauze to the site and apply pressure or have the patient apply pressure. Do not release the patient until the bleeding has stopped.
16. Label the specimen with the proper information.
17. Place a bandage on the site if the patient is over 3 years of age. Tell the patient to leave the bandage on for 30 minutes.
18. Thank the patient when finished.
19. Properly dispose of equipment and supplies.
20. Clean your work area.
21. Remove your gloves and wash your hands.
22. Test, transfer or store the specimen according to your institution's policy.

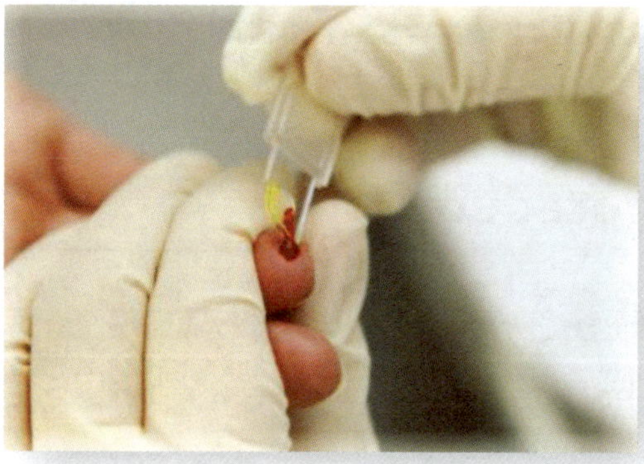

Chapter 6 – Review Questions

MULTIPLE CHOICE:

Select the best response for each of the following questions.

1. __________________ is used to describe the heel bone.

   a. calcaneus
   b. interstitial
   c. palmar
   d. plantar

2. Perform a dermal puncture rather than a venipuncture if:

   a. The patient is an infant or small child
   b. Tests only require a few drops of blood
   c. The patient has fragile veins
   d. All of the above

WORD SCRAMBLE:

Unscramble the word to fill in the blank:

3. **iagicertr**

   __________________ is defined as "pertaining to the elderly".

4. **cealnts**

   __________________ are the most simplest of the skin-puncturing devices. They are composed of a single-use, sterile, disposable metal blade that comes individually wrapped.

5. **piitcropemte**

   __________________ a very small pipette (small tube into which blood is drawn by suction) used in microcollection.

6. **upetnteo**

   An __________________ system is a collection system used for hematology tests used to make accurate dilutions of whole blood.

TRUE OR FALSE:

Indicate if the following statements are true or false.

7. _______ Capillary action is the physical process of blood flowing, or being pulled, into a very thin tube.

8. _______ Occasionally, the sole-side (plantar) surface of the big toe or the earlobe is used as a dermal puncture site.

FILL IN THE BLANKS:

Write the word(s) or statement needed to answer the following questions:

9. List at least two reasons why dermal puncture should not be performed:

____

____

10. What are the two main sites for dermal puncture?

____

____

Chapter 7

Safety in Phlebotomy

Objectives

After completing this chapter, students should be able to:

- Identify rules that promote safety of the individual and patient
- Define principle and procedures of Infection Control
- Recognize proper hand-washing procedures and techniques
- Identify infection and category-specific isolation techniques
- Define Universal Precautions
- Recognize proper handling for precautionary accidental needle punctures
- Define OSHA Standards
- Recognize proper disposal and handling of hazardous materials
- Define Safety Guidelines

Glossary Terms

Asepsis	Free from germs or infection.
Bloodborne Pathogens (BBP)	Infectious organisms found in blood and other body fluids.
Immune	A condition in which the body is able to resist certain illness or toxins.
Nosocomial Infection	Infection that is acquired after a person has entered a hospital caused by the spread of an infection from one person to another.
Occupational Safety And Health Administration (OSHA)	An agency of the U.S. Department of Labor requiring employers to provide a safe work environment including guidelines to protect workers exposed to biological and occupational hazards.
Personal Protective Equipment (PPE)	Protective coverings such as gloves, goggles, gowns, and masks which are worn to minimize exposure to blood and body fluids; they are required by OSHA when handling body fluids.
Sterile	Free of microorganisms.
Susceptible	A condition in which a person is more vulnerable to an illness than normal.

a. Infection Control and Isolation Techniques

1.) Nosocomial Infection

Nosocomial infections are acquired by a patient after admission to a health care facility, such as a hospital, clinic, or nursing home. In an attempt to control nosocomial infections, Infection Control programs have been established which include the following:

- Frequent and proper hand washing
- Use or personal protective equipment (PPE)
- Waste management of contaminated materials
- Use of proper cleaning solutions
- Following standard precautions
- Use of sterile procedures when needed

In order for a nosocomial infection to exist, the chain of infection must be complete. The purpose of Infection Control is to break the chain of infection. The most effective practice to break the chain of infection is hand washing.

The illustration shown below is the key to understanding the chain of infection.

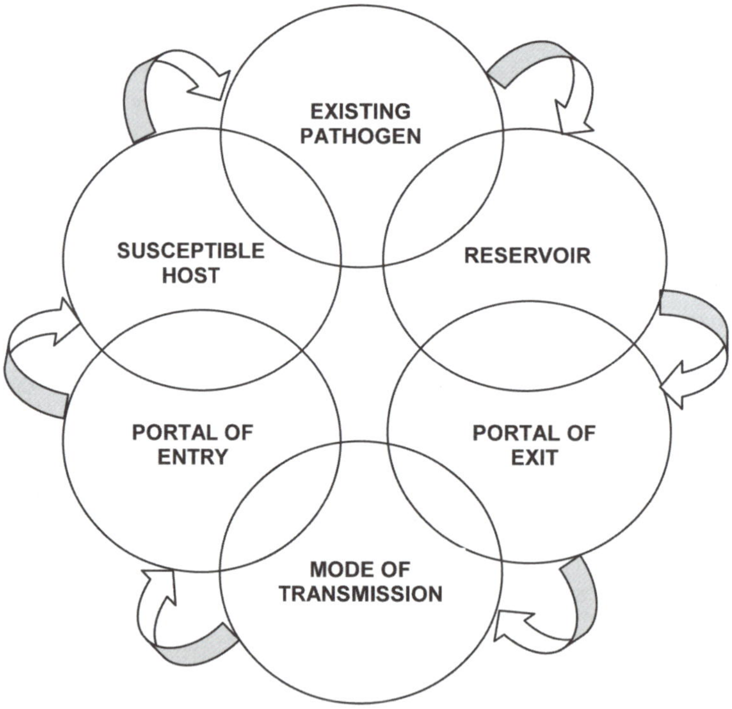

Figure 8.1 Chain of Infection

a. **Existing pathogen** – Disease producing microorganisms.

b. **Reservoir** - The source of the pathogen including individuals who have an illness who may be unaware that they are carriers of disease but can still transmit to another.

c. **Portal of Exit** – The means of escape from the reservoir, including respiratory tract secretions, intestinal waste products, reproductive tract secretions, and blood and blood products),

d. **Mode of Transmission** – Methods of transmission may include improper hand washing, improper isolation techniques, use of disposal equipment, contaminated instruments, and use of facilities. Examples: touching infected individuals, coughing and sneezing and inadequate ventilation.

e. **Portal of Entry** – The means of entry from the reservoir to the new host, such as the respiratory tract, skin and mucous membranes, reproductive and urinary tracts, and blood.

f. **Susceptible Host** – a person who cannot fight off the infection.

2.) Autogenuous Infection

an infection caused by one's own body.

3.) Means of Transmission

can be through direct or indirect contact, airborne transmission, ingestion (i.e. foot, water, etc.).

Transmission of Infection

- Person-to-person contact
- Food-borne infection
- Waterborne infection
- Airborne infection
- Insect-borne infection

4.) Vector-borne

infections are acquired by transmittal of a pathogen from an infected individual to another individual by an arthropod, or other agent. Sometimes animals serve as the intermediary hosts.

b. Procedure for Blood Collection in Isolation Room

Isolation procedures are designed to prevent transmission of infectious agents from patients to staff or visitors, or from staff or visitors to patient. Signs are used outside of patient rooms to indicate isolation precautions. The type of isolation precaution depends on the policies of the health care facility as well as the type of infection.

1. **Strict Isolation** complete isolation used when a patient has a highly contagious disease. Anyone entering the room must wear a gown, mask and gloves. All items taken into the room, such as tube holders, needles and syringes must be disposed of in special containers in the room.
2. **Contact Isolation** – used for patients who have diseases such as influenza, which can be transmitted to another person my means of direct contact. Anyone entering the room should wear a gown, mask and gloves, if they will be in close contact with the patient.
3. **Respiratory Isolation** – used for patients with illnesses which can spread through droplet infection, such as meningoccal meningitis, tuberculosis or measles. Anyone entering the room should wear a gown, mask and gloves.
4. **Tuberculosis Isolation** – patients are placed under AFB isolation precautions for the protection of staff and visitors.
5. **Enteric Precautions** – used for patients who have intestinal infections, such as Salmonella, or hepatitis A and E, which can result in the patient having diarrhea, or dysentery. Anyone entering the room must wear a gown, mask and gloves. All items taken into the room, such as tube holders, needles and syringes must be disposed of in special containers in the room.
6. **Protective or Reverse Isolation** – some hospitals have protective isolation facilities for patients with immune deficiencies; in this type of isolation, patients must live in an environment which is completely sterile. All food and items are sterilized before they are taken into the patient's room.
7. **Universal Blood and Body Fluid Precautions** – using Universal Precautions means that all blood and certain body fluids should be considered potentially infectious for all individuals, and all necessary precautions should be taken to prevent the spread of infection. Infectious fluids include blood, blood products, reproductive secretions, cerebrospinal fluid, synovial fluid, pleural fluid, peritoneal fluid, pericardial fluid, and ammonic fluid. Noninfectious fluids include feces, nasal secretions, sputum, sweat, tears, urine and vomit (not containing blood).

a• Sharps Container

- Dispose of all sharp needles in puncture-resistant waste containers.
- Do not recap needles by hand; do not bend or manipulate used needles by hand.
- Use caution when handling sharp objects, such as needles, or other devices.

b. Standard Precautions

- **Hand Hygiene** - Wash your hands and other skin surfaces immediately and thoroughly after exposure to any type of infectious fluid.
- **Gloves** - Wear gloves when handling chemicals and body fluids, and when touching the non-intact skin of patients. Wear gloves when drawing blood, including finger and heel sticks in infants.
- **PPE** - Use personal protective equipment including gowns, masks, gloves and shields to protect yourself from exposure to blood and other potentially infectious fluids and materials.
- **Patient Care Equipment** – Handle soiled equipment carefully so as to prevent contaminations and transfer to other patients.
- **Environmental Control** – Follow hospital procedures for cleaning beds, equipment and surfaces.
- **Linen** – Handle soiled linen with body fluids carefully so as to prevent personal contamination and transfer to other patients.
- **Occupational Health and Bloodborne Pathogens** - Use care with needles and other sharp objects to avoid injury. Dispose of needles and other sharp objects properly in a puncture-resistant sharps container.

8. **Category-Specific Isolation** - Patients who are recovering from surgical procedures are given drugs that reduce their ability to combat infection and may be kept in a separate section, such as the recovery room. Phlebotomists and health care providers should follow facility guidelines for use of personal protective equipment.
9. **Disease-Specific Isolation** - Some patients who have an infectious disease may be kept in a separate section of a hospital, or other health care facility, such as intensive care. Phlebotomists and health care providers should follow facility guidelines for use of personal protective equipment.

c. OSHA Standards

1.) Exposure Control Plan

OSHA requires that every laboratory have a written Exposure Control Plan. This is used to minimize the employee exposure to infectious materials. In addition, OSHS requires that: The Exposure Control Plan be updated annually. All laboratory personnel review the Exposure Control Plan annually. Records be maintained on each employee regarding hepatitis B vaccination including an exposure incident report. These records must be maintained for the duration of the employment plus 30 years. Records of all training sessions be maintained for 3 years. All employees follow general safety and housekeeping procedures.

2.) Work Practice Controls

After contact with a patient, wash hands thoroughly with either soap and water (if visibly soiled) or with an alcohol-based hand rub (if hands are not visibly soiled).

If your gloves become contaminated with blood, or if they show signs of tears or leaks, change them immediately.

Do not wash or disinfect gloves to reuse because detergents and disinfectants may cause deterioration and because liquids may penetrate through undetected holes.

If you splash blood or other body fluids on your skin or into your mouth or eyes:

1. Wash the area with large amounts of water, followed by appropriate disinfecting agents.
2. Put on gloves and wipe the spill according to your facility's procedures.
3. Record the source patient's name and unique patient identification number.
4. Immediately report the incident to your supervisor.
5. Follow your facility's guidelines regarding treatment and follow-up.

3.) General Methods of Compliance

OSHA was established by the U.S. Congress in 1970 to assure that every employee work in a safe and healthful working environment. OSHA is a federal agency that has the power to enforce regulations concerning the health and safety of employees.

Every laboratory must be aware of OSHA regulations and carefully monitor potential violations. OSHA conducts surprise inspections of workplaces to make sure standards are being met.

4.) Needles and Sharps – Biohazard

As phlebotomists, be sure to use safety devices, such as safety needles, retractable lancet blades, and plastic collection tubes at all times. Do not process specimens sent to the laboratory in an unsafe state, such as a syringe with a needle still attached. Notify your supervisor if you discover any unsafe equipment.

The Needlestick Safety and Prevention Act (2000) and the revised Bloodborne Pathogens Standard (2001) require that:

- health care employees with more than 20 employees maintain a safety log of all injuries caused by needles and sharp objects.
- all safety incidents and accidents be reported to your supervisor.
- all appropriate forms must be completed.

If you stick yourself with a non-sterile sharp device:

1. Remove your gloves and dispose of them properly.
2. Wash the area well with soap and water.
3. Record the source patient's name and unique patient identification number.
4. Immediately report the incident to your supervisor.
5. Follow your facility's guidelines regarding treatment and follow-up.

Remember that all new needles all evacuated blood collection tubes are sterile. When the protecting cover is removed from a new needle, the needle must not touch anything until it punctures the skin. If it touches anything, discard it immediately in an approved puncture-resistant sharps disposal container, and use a new needle and blood tube holder.

5.) Laboratory Techniques

Hand Washing Technique/The 3-Minute Scrub

1. Remove all jewelry.
2. Stand at sink without allowing clothes to touch sink. Turn on water on, using paper towel. Discard paper towel.
3. Wash your hands with antiseptic soap or detergent. Do not use bar soap.
4. Rinse well.
5. Clean your fingernails with a pick.
6. Apply antiseptic soap or detergent to a brush.
7. Using the brush in a downward motion, thoroughly scrub your arms below the elbows, including the wrists, both hands, between the fingers, and the fingertips.
8. Rinse well, holding your hands higher than elbows.
9. Dry, using paper towels. Discard paper towel.
10. Use a paper towel or other material to turn off water taps.

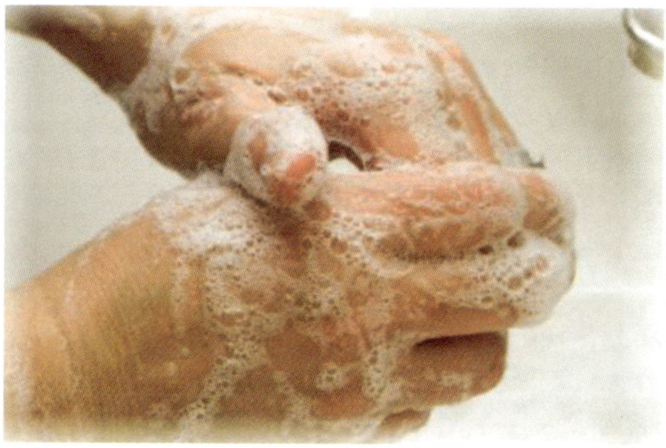

Gown Technique

1. Wash hands thoroughly.
2. Put on a long-sleeve gown with ties in the back.
3. Tie the strings in the back, at the neck and waist.
4. Before removing the gown, wash hands thoroughly again.
5. To remove, untie the neck and then waist of the gown. The gown should be removed and folded with the contaminated side facing inward.
6. Place the folded gown in the specified receptacle.
7. Wash hands once again.

Mask Technique

1. Remove a mask from the box.
2. Place the mask over your nose and mouth.
3. Tie the upper tie high on the head to keep the mask in place, then tie the lower tie.
4. Remove the mask after removing the gown and washing your hands thoroughly.
5. Touch only the strings when removing the mask.
6. Discard the mask in the designated receptacle.

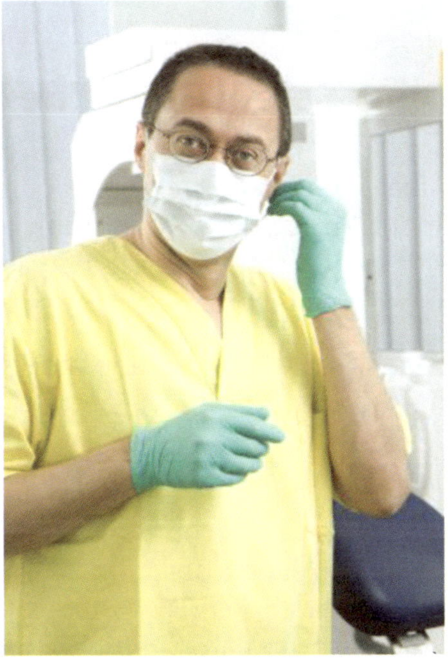

Glove Technique

1. Note that gloves need not be sterile.
2. Pull the ends of the gloves over the sleeves of the gown if a gown is required.
3. Jewelry, such as rings, that might puncture a glove should be removed.
4. Discard gloves after contact with the patient.
5. Wash hands after removing gloves.
6. Note that gloves are worn for all contact with blood and other body fluids.

d. Disposal of Used Materials

1. **Medical Waste** – includes solid waste (paper goods, bottles, cans, etc.), chemical waste (germicides, cleaning solvents and pharmaceutical drugs), radioactive waste (waste than contains or is contaminated with liquid or solid radioactive material), and infectious waste (laboratory cultures, blood, and blood products which may carry disease).

   For treating infectious waste, it is sometimes necessary to alter the waster in order to render it non-infectious. Methods for treating infectious waste include incineration, chemical treatment, and steam sterilization. For the latter method, an autoclave is used to saturate waste with high-temperature steam.

e. Importance of Following Safety Guidelines

As phlebotomists, it is critical that safety guidelines be followed at all times. Set a goal to master safety information and skills to minimize risks to your health, and the health of patients. As advancing in technology offer increasing methods of safety in healthcare, it is up to you to practice good techniques and use common sense in daily practice.

Always remember to follow general safety rules in laboratory settings. General guidelines include the following:

- Walk, never run in a laboratory.
- Never carry or handle uncapped syringes, needles or sharp instruments.
- Keep floors clean. Clean spills promptly or contact housekeeping staff to assist.
- Report all unsafe conditions to you supervisor at once.
- Never eat, drink or smoke in a laboratory.
- Never store any personal items in a laboratory refrigerator.
- Never apply lipstick, make-up or contact lenses in a laboratory.
- Never place anything in your mouth, such as a pencil while in a laboratory.
- Wear personal protective equipment (PPE) as required.
- Wear shoes which cover the entire foot.
- Keep all chemicals below eye level in case a spill occurs.
- Avoid wearing loose clothing, such as a scarf, which can become tangled with equipment.
- If an emergency occurs, keep calm, remove all patients from the area as required, and be sure to follow all emergency procedures for the facility.

Chapter 7 – Review Questions

MULTIPLE CHOICE:

Select the best response for each of the following questions.

1. _________________ are infectious organisms found in blood and other body fluids.

   e. asepsis
   f. hosts
   g. bloodborne pathogens
   h. nosocomials

2. _________________ is a condition in which a person is more vulnerable to an illness than normal.

   i. airborne
   j. pathogenic
   k. immune
   l. susceptible

WORD SCRAMBLE:

Unscramble the word to fill in the blank:

3. **muniem**

   _________________ is a condition in which the body is able to resist certain illness or toxins.

4. **tileres**

   _________________ means free of microorganisms.

5. **inoolisat**

   _________________ procedures are designed to prevent transmission of infectious agents from patients to staff or visitors, or from staff or visitors to patient.

6. **HASO**

   _________________ was established by the U.S. Congress in 1970 to assure that every employee work in a safe and healthful working environment.

TRUE OR FALSE:

Indicate if the following statements are true or false.

7. _______ Personal protective equipment (PPE) are not required by OSHA when handling body fluids.

8. _______ Nosocomial infections are acquired by a patient after admission to a health care facility, such as a hospital, clinic, or nursing home.

9. _______ An autogenuous infection can be caused by one's own body

FILL IN THE BLANKS:

Write the word(s) or statement needed to answer the following question:

10. What is medical waste?

____

____

Chapter 8

Complications in Phlebotomy

Objectives

After completing this chapter, students should be able to:

- Identify complications and patient reactions which may occur during and after venipuncture
- Recognize hemolysis during venous collection
- Define hemoconcentration
- Recognize how to handle the uncooperative patient
- Describe methods used to prevent complications

Glossary Terms

Anaphylactic	Severe allergic reaction.
Hematoma	Swelling caused by leakage of blood into tissues due to a break in the blood vessel.
Hemoconcentration	A rapid increase in the ratio of blood components (cells) to plasma (liquid).
Hemolysis	the destruction of red blood cells.
Lymphostatis	Lack of fluid drainage in the lymph system, usually caused by lymph node removal.
Syncope	Fainting.

Many complications can occur during venipuncture , including nerve damage, artery puncture, hematoma formation, and skin infection. As phlebotomists, it is important to be aware of these complications as well as practice proper procedures for prevention.

a. Nerve Damage

Never use the anterior or palm side of the wrist or hand to collect a blood specimen. Doing so may increase the risk of hitting a nerve because of nerve locations close to the skin's surface.

Permanent nerve damage can occur from:

- Poor site selection
- Movement of patient during needle insertion
- Insertion of needle too deeply or quickly
- Blind probing

b. Artery Puncture

If you accidentally puncture an artery, apply pressure to the site for 5 full minutes after removing the needle, then apply a pressure bandage. A pressure bandage can be made by folding a two-by-two inch gauze twice to quarter it. Place the gauze on the venipuncture site and then apply a bandage.

c. If Bleeding Doesn't Stop

If the patient has a low platelet count, a bleeding disorder, or is on anticoagulation therapy, the blood flow may not readily stop. In these cases, instruct the patient to elevate his or her arm above shoulder level, and apply pressure for 5 to 10 minutes or more. When the bleeding has stopped, apply a folded gauge pad and adhesive bandage, and inform the patient to not use the affected extremity for a short time, and avoid strenuous activity for 24 hours.

If the bleeding continues, maintain pressure on the site and contact your supervisor for help. Do not leave the patient until the situation is under control.

d. Fainting

If a patient has a history of fainting, lay them down to perform the venipuncture. If the patient does not have a history of fainting, but faints in the phlebotomy chair, or in another seated position:

- Stop the procedure and ask for assistance (be sure to remove the tourniquet and needle as soon as possible).
- Lower the patient's head to their knees.
- Place a cold compress or washcloth on the patient's forehead and on the back of the neck.
- Hold the patient in the chair.
- Contact the physician if the patient doesn't respond.
- Keep the patient in the area for at least 15 minutes after he or she has recovered, before you release him or her.
- Observe the patient after he or she stands following the procedure.
- Inform your supervisor and complete an incident report if needed.

e. Hematoma

Hematoma occurs when blood leaks into the tissues during or after blood collection. It is the most common complication of venipuncture.

If hematoma occurs during venipuncture:

- Release the tourniquet immediately.
- Withdraw the needle.
- Apply pressure on the site for at least 2 minutes.
- Apply cold compresses to reduce the pain and swelling.

Hematoma may also occur after blood collection. After the venipuncture, do not instruct the patient to bend their arm. This will cause the wound to remain open, causing blood to escape into tissues, which may result in a bruise or hematoma.

To prevent hematomas:

- Do not use a vein which is too small for the needle.
- Be careful to make sure the needle is only partially inserted into the vein.
- Do not probe blinding excessively to find a vein.
- Do not remove the needle while the tourniquet is still on.
- Be sure to apply adequate pressure to the site after venipuncture.

f. Hemoconcentration

Hemoconcentration, the increase in red blood cells and other cells and solids in the blood, is caused from loss of fluid in the surrounding tissues around the venipuncture site. This may be due to one the following, which should be avoided:

- Leaving the tourniquet on for too long
- Excessive massaging, squeezing or probing of the venipuncture site
- Long-term IV therapy
- Occluded (closed or constricted) veins

g. Hemolysis

Hemosysis can be caused by improper phlebotomy techniques, such as using a needle which is too small, collecting the blood too quickly into a tube, shaking or mixing tubes vigorously, or performing venipuncture before the alcohol has dried on the site. As phlebotomists, it is important to be careful and follow procedures at all times, in an effort to prevent hemolysis.

h. Skin Infection

Follow the following antiseptic techniques to avoid skin infection:

- Do not touch the site after cleansing
- Remove the needle cap at the last possible minute prior to blood collection
- Do no open bandages ahead of time

i. Allergies

In the event that a patient is allergic to supplies used during venipuncture, an allergic reaction may occur. This may range from a mild skin infection to a life-threatening anaphylactic shock.

As phlebotomists, it is important to check all patient records to make sure there are no documented patient allergies. If a patient has a known allergy to iodine, an alternative antiseptic should be used, such as soap and water.

Some patients may also be allergic to the adhesive found in bandages. As an alternative, use sterile gauze folded into a square and adhere with hypoallergenic tape.

Latex is also a common cause for allergic reactions. If a patient is allergic to latex, it is important that no latex products are brought into the patient room. Instead of latex products, vinyl gloves and tourniquets with velcro closure may be used.

It is possible for any patient to have a reaction, so be prepared every time you do a venipuncture.

j. Pain

Patients who are anxious are more likely to experience pain. Prior to venipuncture, it is important to reduce stress and tension in the patient. Calmly explain the procedure to the patient to alleviate the patient's fears.

Be sure not to excessively probe the venipuncture site blindly, which can be extremely painful, as well as damaging to veins and nerves.

Remember to let the alcohol dry on the site before beginning the procedure. If the alcohol is not completely evaporated, it may cause a stinging sensation.

k. The Uncooperative Patient

If the patient is too old or too young to understand what is going on, do not attempt the venipuncture alone. Obtain help from a nurse, fellow phlebotomist, or family member.

If the patient is mentally disturbed, mentally impaired, or suffering from substance abuse, be sure to reassure the patient. If the patient will not cooperate, seek assistance prior to performing the venipuncture.

If the patient if of sound mind, but refuses to cooperate, explain to the patient that the physician has ordered the blood tests to properly manage the patient's health and prescribe medicine.

Ultimately, if the patient refuses blood collection, document it on the requisition form and inform the patient's nurse of the situation.

Chapter 8 – Review Questions

MULTIPLE CHOICE:

Select the best response for each of the following questions.

1. A __________________ is swelling caused by leakage of blood into tissues due to a break in the blood vessel.

   a. hematoma b. hemoconcentration
   c. hemolysis d. lymphostatis

2. __________________ is a complication which can occur during venipuncture.

   a. nerve damage b. leuckopenia
   c. skin infection d. both a. and c.

WORD SCRAMBLE:

Unscramble the word to fill in the blank:

3. **ticanalacphy**

   __________________ can be defined as a severe allergic reaction.

4. **pcoynes**

   __________________ is another word for fainting.

5. **sihsyosem**

   __________________ can be caused by improper phlebotomy techniques, such as using a needle which is too small, collecting the blood too quickly into a tube, shaking or mixing tubes vigorously, or performing venipuncture before the alcohol has dried on the site.

6. **xaelt**

   __________________ is also a common cause for allergic reactions.

TRUE OR FALSE:

Indicate if the following statements are true or false.

7. ________ Do not collecting a blood specimen on the anterior or palm side of the wrist or hand because this may increase the risk of nerve damage.

8. ________ Patients who are anxious are more likely to experience pain.

FILL IN THE BLANKS:

Write the word(s) or statement needed to answer the following questions:

9. Hemoconcentration, the increase in red blood cells and other cells and solids in the blood, is caused from loss of fluid in the surrounding tissues around the venipuncture site. List two reasons why this may occur:

____

____

10. List three way to avoid skin infection:

____

____

____

____

Chapter 9

Special Specimen Collection

Objectives

After completing this chapter, students should be able to:

- Discuss the importance of timed specimens
- Explain glucose testing
- Identify standard procedures for blood donation
- Identify factors that affect laboratory specimens
- Differentiate between forensic and toxicology specimens

Glossary Terms

Analyte	A substance undergoing analysis, such as glucose or cholesterol.
Diabetes Mellitus	A condition in which the patient has impaired carbohydrate metabolism due to deficiency of insulin.
Lipemic	Serum or plasma which is cloudy, caused by increased lipids.
Polycythemia	A condition that causes an overproduction or abnormal increase in the number of red blood cells.
Postprandial	After eating a meal.
QNS (Quantity Not Sufficient)	Specimen amount is too small to perform the test ordered.
Stat	immediately.

In addition to performing routine blood collection, phlebotomists may also be required to perform special laboratory tests. These may include timed specimens, glucose tolerance tests, blood donation collection, and therapeutic collection.

a. Timed Specimens

A laboratory requisition will frequently state the time a blood specimen should be drawn. A specimen collection may be timed due to:

- therapeutic medication blood levels
- changes in a patient's condition
- the need to measure the patient's ability to metabolize a substance
- the need to measure analytes that exhibit diurnal variation (daily fluctuations)

As phlebotomists, it is important to understand why patient preparation before blood collection, as well as timing of the collection is critical to a patient's well-being. Laboratory tests which are collected at specific times include peak and trough medication levels for drug monitoring, 2-hour post prandial tests, glucose level tests, glucose tolerance tests, iron level tests, hormone lab analyses, cortisol level tests, and cardiac enzyme tests.

Stat specimens, which may be ordered to treat a critically ill patient, must be resulted as soon as possible. If you receive a stat laboratory requisition, draw the blood immediately, making sure to use proper care and proper procedures. After collecting the specimen, deliver it to the laboratory promptly.

A fasting specimen requires that the patient abstain from food and beverages (except for water), for 8 to 12 hours prior to having their blood drawn. The most common tests requiring fasting are cholesterol, triglycerides, and glucose determinations.

If the patient has not fasted for a blood test which requires fasting, check with your supervisor to determine if the blood should be drawn.

b. Glucose Testing

Glucose testing is one of the most frequently ordered laboratory test. Testing glucose levels assists in the diagnosis of diabetes mellitus, gestational diabetes, and other related glucose abnormalities. Diabetes mellitus is a condition in which the patient has impaired carbohydrate metabolism due to deficiency of insulin. Hypoglycemia is a related condition where the amount of sugar in the blood is too low. Both blood and urine samples are taken at periodic intervals to determine how long it takes for the patient to metabolize the glucose.

The 2-hour postprandial glucose test screens for diabetes and takes place 2 hours after eating. Two to three days prior to the test, the patient is instructed to eat a diet high in carbohydrates. The morning of the test, the patient is to eat a breakfast containing 100 g glucose. Two hours later, the patient's blood is drawn for testing. If the patient's glucose level is abnormally high, a more specific test called the glucose tolerance test is administered.

During a glucose tolerance test (GTT), a loading dose of glucose is given to the patient to drink.

The phlebotomist must make sure that all the glucose solution is swallowed within 5 minutes. For a 3-hour GTT, blood specimens are drawn at 30 minutes, 1 hour, 2 hours, and 3 hours after the loading dose of glucose was administered. Urine samples are also collected at these times. During the test, the patient cannot have any food or drink, except water.

A phlebotomist is required to give the patient instructions as well as collecting the specimens at the appropriate times. With all timed tests, timing is critical. If blood is collected too early, the patient's glucose level may still be elevated; this may lead to misinterpretation of the rest results.

c. Blood Donation Collection

Blood donation collection is another common procedure which phlebotomist may need to perform. This may be for American Red Cross centers, community blood centers, or hospital collection centers.

Phlebotomists who collect blood from volunteer donors should possess excellent skills in venipuncture an interpersonal communication. It is critical that every phase of the blood donation collection be performed smoothly and professionally.

Individuals who donate blood must have their medical history screened and checked. This includes checking the frequency of previous donations, past and present medications, exposure to diseases, recent vaccinations, and foreign travel. Donors must also have the following checked:

- blood pressure
- temperature
- weight (must be at least 110 lbs.)
- age (must be between 17 and 66)
- pulse
- general health and appearance
- hemoglobin or hemocrit

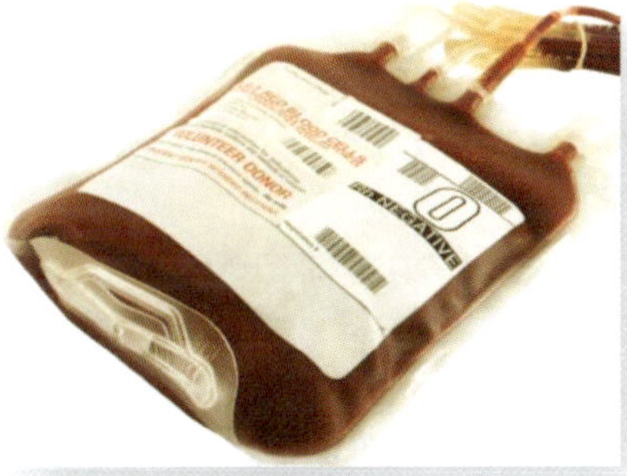

The step-by-step procedure for blood donation collection is as follows:

1. After the donor passes the history and medical screening and is comfortably seated in a phlebotomy chair or bed, locate a suitable vein.
2. Prepare the site.
3. Prepare the blood collection bag and scale. Be sure there is a clamp between the bag and the needle.
4. Apply the tourniquet or blood pressure cuff, and give the patient something to squeeze (to expand the vein).
5. Perform the venipuncture.
6. Release the clamp. If there is a steady flow of blood into the bag, tape the needle to the arm.
7. Cover the area with sterile gauze. Do not leave the patient during the drawing process.
8. Have the patient unclench their fist, then release the tourniquet or blood pressure cuff.
9. When the amount of blood (approximately 450 ml) is collected, be sure the donor has stopped clenching their fist, then clamp or tie a knot in the tubing.
10. Collect pilot tubes before removing the needle from the donor's arm. Pilot tubes are samples of donor blood to be tested before the unit is released for transfusion.
11. Strip the tubing and thoroughly mix the blood, then allow the tubing to refill.
12. Place the units in storage as directed by your supervisor.
13. Do not allow the patient to leave unless the bleeding has stopped and at least 10 minutes have elapsed. Instruct the patient to increase fluid intake over the next 24 hours, avoid alcohol until after a meal, and avoid smoking for at least 30 minutes.
14. Always be polite, courteous and professional. Strive to have the patient leave with a positive feeling so that they may be inclined to donate blood again.

d. Therapeutic Collection

Therapeutic phlebotomy is the intentional collection of a large volume of blood. Therapeutic blood collection may be performed due to various medical reasons, such as to relieve stress on the body due to overproduction of iron or red blood cells. It is also commonly used to treat polycythemia, which causes an increase production of red blood cells, as well as hemochromatosis, which causes the body to store abnormally large amount of iron.

Therapeutic blood collection is performed the same way a blood donation would be performed. Usually, 500 ml are taken during one treatment. Patients are then closely monitored. The blood collected is not suitable for blood transfusion and is therefore discarded.

e. Blood Culture Collection

The rate of isolation of micro-organisms from blood is directly related to the volume of blood collected. Therefore, it is recommended that a blood culture set consist of a total 30 mL (for adults) and less than 10 mL for pediatrics collected from two separate venipuncture sites.

The bottles making up the set should be collected at the same time.

It is critical that there be meticulous preparation of the skin prior to venipuncture to prevent contamination of the specimen which could result in inappropriate antimicrobial therapy.

f. Forensic and Toxicology Specimens

Although most blood tests are ordered by physicians for medical reasons, they are sometimes needed for legal reasons. Forensic specimens may be needed for evidence in legal proceedings. Blood samples collected for forensic evidence may include alcohol level tests, drug screenings and blood for DNA analysis. Phlebotomists must follow a specific protocol that documents the location of the specimen at all times as well as who has access to it, from the collection until the time of the final result. This process if called chain of custody.

Blood collected for alcohol level tests should be collected using a gray top evacuated tube that contains sodium fluoride. Alcohol wipes should not be used to cleanse the skin for this type of test because residual alcohol may contaminate the sample and produce erroneous results.

Toxicology specimens may be needed for the scientific study of poisons, drugs, or medications. They may be ordered by toxicologists, who study the detection of poisons, the action of poisons on the human body, and the treatment of the medical conditions poisons can cause. It is critical to follow your laboratory's protocol when collecting toxicology specimens. Oil or bacteria from hands or materials may contaminate or react with some analytes, which are substances undergoing analysis, such as glucose or cholesterol.

g. Factors That Affect Blood Specimens

Phlebotomists must be aware of the many factors which can affect laboratory test results including the following:

- Potassium, phosphorus, enzyme levels and lactate blood levels can be affected by prolonged use of a tourniquet (over 1 minute).
- The dietary state of the patient can affect the outcome of a test result. If a test required fasting, it is the responsibility of the phlebotomist that this be checked in order to determine if the patient is properly prepared for blood collection.
- If the incorrect volume of blood is drawn, this can affect test results. Too much blood in some tubes will cause clotting. When not enough blood is collected, the specimen is QNS (quantity not sufficient).
- The order of draw is critical for accurate test results. If an EDTA tube is drawn before a citrate tube, for example, the PT and APTT results will be erroneously increased.
- If tests require that blood samples be chilled, such as ammonia, be sure not to delay chilling will can alter the test results.
- Improper timing of specimen collection. The exat time of specimen collection must be noted on the specimen label.
- Wrong tube used.
- Shaking a blood filled tube can cause hemolyses
- Vigorous pumping of the hand can falsely elevate potassium phosphorus and lactate blood levels.

Chapter 9 – Review Questions

MULTIPLE CHOICE:

Select the best response for each of the following questions.

1. __________________ is a condition that causes an overproduction or abnormal increase in the number of red blood cells.

   a. diabetes mellitus
   b. polycythemia
   c. leukocytosis
   d. leuckopenia

2. Stat specimens must be resulted:

   a. within 1 hour
   b. as soon as possible
   c. at the next schedule collection time
   d. within 24 hours

WORD SCRAMBLE:

Unscramble the word to fill in the blank:

3. **lyantea**

   A __________________ is a substance undergoing analysis, such as glucose or cholesterol.

4. **miliecp**

   __________________ is serum or plasma which is cloudy, caused by increased lipids.

5. **ranosptalpdi**

   __________________ means after eating a meal.

6. **siromeochtosmah**

   __________________ causes the body to store abnormally large amount of iron.

TRUE OR FALSE:

Indicate if the following statements are true or false.

7. ________ Phlebotomists must follow a specific protocol that documents the location of the specimen at all times as well as who has access to it, from the collection until the time of the final result. This process if called transition protocol.

8. ________ Glucose testing is one of the most frequently ordered laboratory test.

FILL IN THE BLANKS:

Write the word(s) or statement needed to answer the following questions:

9. List 2 reasons why a specimen may be timed:

____

____

10. Donors must have their blood pressure, temperature and pulse checked. In addition, they must be at least ____________ lbs. and they must be between ____________ and ____________ years old.

Appendix A - Laboratory Seek-n-Find Puzzle

T	E	L	C	E	T	T	G	C	0	L	E	D	E	I	T	H	R	D	I
I	L	A	R	E	Y	H	N	H	S	F	I	B	R	I	N	0	G	E	N
P	E	A	0	H	P	M	E	E	I	E	I	I	T	0	U	B	E	E	S
0	S	M	S	N	E	L	A	M	A	I	T	N	N	0	I	M	R	U	S
T	S	I	S	F	S	R	0	I	A	E	0	0	E	L	E	U	N	D	A
N	P	C	M	A	H	B	I	S	E	T	0	E	I	L	B	E	C	R	F
N	E	R	A	S	A	0	E	T	C	P	0	R	R	E	0	0	H	A	E
E	E	0	T	T	R	A	I	R	E	I	U	L	L	B	A	S	0	Z	T
E	H	S	C	I	P	S	C	Y	U	B	A	L	0	A	F	I	L	A	Y
D	E	C	H	N	S	G	M	T	I	T	A	A	S	G	E	N	E	H	C
L	P	0	L	G	E	N	L	N	A	R	C	0	0	0	Y	0	S	0	T
E	A	P	P	I	P	A	T	I	E	N	T	N	T	S	T	P	T	I	N
P	T	E	P	L	A	T	E	L	E	T	U	G	U	S	L	H	E	B	E
S	I	T	I	R	0	U	G	L	U	C	0	S	E	P	E	I	R	0	0
A	T	H	E	0	S	E	A	N	E	M	I	A	H	0	I	L	0	U	N
R	I	Y	D	T	S	C	0	A	G	U	L	A	T	I	0	N	L	B	A
C	S	R	R	N	E	0	S	E	D	S	L	I	D	E	A	H	E	I	T
S	H	0	U	S	E	R	0	L	0	G	Y	S	E	R	U	M	I	V	A
D	I	I	G	S	T	A	P	H	Y	L	0	C	0	C	C	U	S	T	L
G	R	D	L	Y	R	N	U	R	I	N	A	L	Y	S	I	S	H	P	L

FIND THESE WORDS ASSOCIATED WITH THE LABORATORY

ANEMIA
BILIRUBIN
BIOHAZARD
CHEMISTRY
CHOLESTEROL
COAGULATION
CROSSMATCH
DRUG
EOSINOPHIL
FASTING
FIBRINOGEN
GLUCOSE
HEMATOLOGY
HEPATITIS
MICROSCOPE
NEEDLE
NEONATAL
PATIENT
PLATELET
RUBELLA
SAFETY
SEROLOGY
SERUM
SHARPS
SLIDE
STAPHYLOCOCCUS
THYROID
TYPE
URINALYSIS
VENIPUNCTURE

Appendix B – Sample Patient Scripts

Sample Inpatient Identification Script

SAMPLE
IN-PATIENT IDENTIFICATION
SCRIPT

Knock on door, enter and greet the patient.

Greeting: "Good morning, how are you this morning?"
"My name is Sara and I'm from the lab. Dr. Jones has ordered some lab work for you today so I will need to take a sample of blood from you. Do you have any questions or concerns?"

Patient answers

"Before we get started, I need to have you tell me your full name and your date of birth.
Could you spell your last name for me please?"

Patient gives name and date of birth while phlebotomist verifies name and date of birth with the requisition labels and then matches that information with the hospital id wristband.

Patient spell last name

Thank you. Now we can get started."

SAMPLE
OUT- PATIENT IDENTIFICATION
SCRIPT

Phlebotomist goes to the waiting room and calls patient by first name. (Do not give last name, HIIPA).

Calling patient and greeting: "Jane. Good morning, my name is Sara. Would you follow me please? You may have a seat here.

"Jane, Dr. Jones has ordered a lipid profile and cbc for you today. The lipid profile requires you to be fasting for 10-12 hours. Have you had anything to eat or drink during this period?"

Patient answers

Patient identification: "Jane I will need to have you tell me your last name, spell it, and give me your date of birth."

Patient responds

"Jane, do you have any questions before we get started?"

Patient responds

"Let's begin."